A GERRY ANDERSON

5 STAR 5

JOHN LOVELL AND THE ZARGON THREAT

BY RICHARD JAMES

Based on an original screenplay by
Gerry Anderson and Tony Barwick

ANDERSON
ENTERTAINMENT

Anderson Entertainment Limited
The Corner House, 2 High Street, Aylesford, Kent, ME20 7BG

Hardback edition published in 2021.
Paperback edition published in 2022.

www.gerryanderson.com

ISBN: 978-1-914522-36-9

Editorial director: Jamie Anderson
Cover design: Marcus Stamps

Typeset by Rajender Singh Bisht

TABLE OF CONTENTS

FOREWORD

I n 1977, riding high on the success of his TV series, Space: 1999, producer Gerry Anderson began fundraising to bring a movie to life. Five Star Five had the potential to mark Anderson's debut proper on the big screen (previous cinematic projects had played as second feature to larger films). He engaged writer Tony Barwick, with whom he already had a working relationship from series such as Thunderbirds, Captain Scarlet and UFO, to produce a script described as 'The Magnificent Seven in space'.

Pre-production began in 1979, with stages booked at Pinewood and Bray. Ultimately, despite the involvement of noted director John Guillermin (The Towering Inferno, Death on the Nile) and designer Keith Wilson (UFO, Space: 1999), the project collapsed when funding fell through.

We'll never know just how successful the film would have been. With the newly released Star Wars changing the cinematic landscape, perhaps the world would have been ready for a wise-cracking freighter captain and his chimpanzee side kick. Or perhaps it would have been lost in the slew of science fiction and fantasy movies released in the late Seventies, desperate to emulate George Lucas' extraordinary success. Either way, as you'll see, Five Star Five was yet another example of Gerry Anderson dreaming big.

In adapting the script, I kept the story as near to the original screenplay as I could. I am mindful that this novelisation is almost an historical document, the nearest thing any of us will actually get to seeing the film, so I was careful not to take too many liberties. Tony Barwick's comedic touches have survived (alongside a few of my own), as has Gerry Anderson's distinctive brand of explosive action.

Richard James, 2021

I

INCURSION

The purple sky split with a crack. The troop carrier dropped from the clouds to the ground, slicing through the rain to the ocean beneath. It rose and fell with the waves, never more than a few feet from the water's surface. Sleek and foreboding, it screamed to the shore and hugged the contours of the mountain range beyond. Its engines roared at the limits of their tolerance as the craft banked sharply into a valley, dropping like a stone to follow the lie of the land. Faster than sound, it veered onto a level plain, streaking across the horizon like a bullet. Suddenly, it pulled out into a narrow valley, the peaks on either side accentuating the already sickening sense of speed. Its forward hull glowed a fierce red as it sliced through the atmosphere, scissor wings tucked back in the pursuit of yet more acceleration.

Inside, the movement was barely perceptible. The carrier's inertial dampeners kept the interior stable as it screamed along the alien terrain. Only occasionally could the twelve assembled raiders feel a gentle swoop as they rose and fell. The screech of the engines was dulled, on the inside at least, to a gentle, almost soothing hum.

Leutna Braxx looked about him. As his gaze fell upon each of his team in turn, his heads-up visor displayed their names and vital signs. Smitz, Keral and Boon sat opposite. The Leutna could tell they were tense. They each had an elevated heart rate and raised levels of stress hormones. He knew they'd cope. Like every other shock troop in the vehicle, they had trained hard. The Leutna was careful to give nothing away. His troopers looked to him for leadership. If he betrayed any sign of emotion at their impending mission, it could spell disaster. He clenched his jaw, his face impassive.

The shock troops' combat gear threw bizarre shadows on the wall behind them. Pipes led from their helmets to self-contained air supplies on their backs. Communication packs nestled on their chests. The sheer black material of their hazard suits reflected the lights from the cockpit. A subtle shift in gravity spoke of a sudden acceleration, and the craft banked away to avoid the Kestran surveillance beams. The Leutna cast a glance towards the cockpit. The pilot sat, impassive, his hands gripped on the stick controls. Leutna Braxx knew he was doing very little actual piloting. The craft's systems were following a predetermined course. Every rock and outcrop had been mapped and fed into its guidance systems so that its computer could plot the safest course. The pilot was merely there as a fail-safe. Braxx grunted to himself. Despite all the technology, he felt more secure with a real pair of hands at the controls.

Through the tinted windshield, Kestra's surface was a blur. Multi-coloured crystalline rock formations flashed past. To the east, the Leutna saw a large area of smooth rock. Fissures in the escarpment led to a swampy area. In the middle, a small island was nestled like a bird on a nest. As the carrier swung towards it, hugging the terrain to evade detection, Braxx saw a tall, circular tower brandishing an array of revolving and fixed antennae. He heard a beep from the cockpit console, and the pilot turned to the troops behind him.

'There it is,' he barked, his voice harsh and grating through his comms. 'Kestra's Southern Early Warning System. Get ready.'

Leutna Braxx nodded to his team and, as one, they pressed a button on the sides of their helmets. Their visors tinted as each of their HU displays flickered to life. Only now were they allowed to see the details of the mission. Information scrolled before them. Analysis of the terrain, the nature of the target, odds of success. The Leutna felt his team tense as they read, but he had faith their training would see them through. The white strip lighting above them flicked to red in readiness of the mission. A cacophony of alarms and indicators bleeped from the pilot's console.

The craft's wings extended as it reduced speed and, with a hiss, it began its descent. Crossing over an enormous crystalline boulder, the troop carrier came to rest near a muddy pool on the island. Almost immediately, it was silent. For a moment it sat, exuding a brooding menace. Above it, the sky was turning a lustrous vermillion as the sun set. Kestra's five moons hung low on the horizon. Then, with a hum, the de-planing ramps began to slide from the vehicle's hull. After a pause, Leutna Braxx led his raiders onto the planet's surface, waving them on to shelter behind a crystalline escarpment. As he peered through his visor, his HUD displayed the names and vital signs of each of his troops in turn. Otherwise, in their tight black fatigues, they would be completely indistinguishable. They held their Heat Exchanger Guns at shoulder height in readiness. Light grenades were fixed to their utility belts. As he joined them in readiness, Braxx pressed his back against the rock and cast a glance at the scene before him. Beyond the troop carrier, he could see the silhouette of the electronic surveillance station. Their target was in sight. His HUD picked out some of the local flora and labelled it; *Aquaflora Linguista*. The details scrolled before him. *Swamp Plant. Height: Four feet. Foliage: Bright yellow and exotic multi-coloured flowers.* Braxx waved his hand impatiently and the information disappeared.

Raising a fist to be sure he had everyone's attention, Leutna Braxx indicated that the troopers should move forwards towards a shallow fissure in the rock. He knew from his briefing that it led around the craft to emerge only metres from the target. The squad nodded in understanding and moved off. Braxx noticed Smitz brush against one of the strange flowers and, suddenly, his HUD flashed red. Danger.

As Smitz reached out to push the plant away, its petals contracted as if in pain. The leaves on its stem began to spasm as the troops looked on. Suddenly, from somewhere deep within the flowerhead, there came a scream. It was a loud piercing screech of distress that rose into the air about them. Panicked, the troopers threw themselves to the ground. They couldn't risk being discovered this close to their target. As they looked to their Leutna for instructions, the scream subsided to a series of childlike sobs. After a moment more, the flower seemed to relax. Its petals opened and its stem straightened. The pain had clearly passed. Braxx shook his head. If he got through this, he would be sure to update the mysterious plant's entry in his databanks.

The Leutna nodded to his team and they rose from the ground as one. At a signal, they continued their progress through the fissure, being extra careful to avoid the clumps of strange foliage. Skirting around their craft, the squad emerged onto a swampy plain. Wisps of vapour drifted aimlessly above the slick of black water. Clumps of purple rushes rose from the surface. On the firmer ground that rose here and there, Braxx's HUD indicated more of the strange, screaming plants. Knowing it was the quickest way to the target, the Leutna took a breath, held his HE Gun above his head and led his team into the swamp.

The water rose above their knees as they waded carefully between the plants with barely a sound. As they neared an area of solid ground beyond the swamp, the small battalion could see their way was blocked. A bank of *Aquaflora Linguista* rose before them, seemingly impenetrable. Troopers Keral and Boon took it upon themselves to investigate further. As the light faded around them, they waded along the rampart of plants, looking for a way through. Finally, they were rewarded with the sight of a deep gully leading between two banks of flora. They waved to their squad. Braxx nodded and motioned to his team that they should follow. Keeping low in the water, they each took their turn to navigate the gulley, being careful not to touch the plants on either side. To brush against one might panic those around it, too. Braxx breathed deep. There must be hundreds of the things. Enough to cause quite a commotion.

As the raiders pressed on before him, he could see the area ahead was choked with the plants. With a wink of an eye he pulled up his team manifest. The names scrolled before him. Each of them showed an increase in blood pressure. Their hearts were racing. Dismissing the list with a wave of his hand, he peered ahead to where Keral and Boon were leading the way. They were stretching up, trying to make themselves thin enough to evade the fronds that reached towards them from the bank. At the front of the line, Boon was confronted by a particularly thick growth that blocked his path. He looked back to the Leutna. He knew he had no choice if they were to proceed. Carefully, he pushed against the main stem of one of the plants, gently bending it back. A gap widened, large enough for the troopers to pass through. Each of them in turn held the stem gently as they passed by. From his position at the group's rear, Braxx looked up to the tower ahead. He could just make out one or two Kestran guards patrolling its perimeter, their outlines picked out in red by his Heads Up Display. Lowering his gaze, Braxx was just in time to notice that his time had come to pass through the gully. Except he had neglected to take a hold of the flower stem before him. It slapped against his visor with a fleshy *thwack* and then seemed to draw itself back as if stunned. Braxx's HUD flashed red. He knew what was coming.

The Electronic Surveillance Station was in night mode. The interior lights had dimmed to an approximation of dusk. Having been relieved by their replacements, groups of Kestran guards made their way to the canteen, their day's work done. Still, the control room was a hive of activity. The circular space was filled with electronic equipment and consoles. Before them sat the Kestran operatives, their slender fingers dancing across the keyboards. Only their casual dress and almond shaped eyes marked them out as any different to the Zargon raiders making their way, unseen, below. The hum of conversation filled the air, interrupted at intervals by voices that crackled from the desk mounted comms units. Other surveillance stations were checking in or sharing information. In a less cluttered area, a group of guards had settled at a table to play Kestran Poker. They were in for a long night but, if it was like every other night before it, an uneventful one.

Several storeys up, an observation platform encircled the tower. A guard leaned lazily against the metal fencing that ran the length of the platform. She had slept all day in readiness for her night shift and was struggling to shake off the heaviness in her limbs. She rubbed her face and gave a yawn, letting her gaze wander to the moons on the horizon. Stretching her arms, she moved along the perimeter, her footsteps momentarily breaking the silence. Just as she turned the corner, she heard a familiar scream from the swamp below. She shook her head. No doubt a Kestran Gumbac had just run into one of the native screech flowers. Giving the sound no further thought, the guard leaned back against the tower wall to wish the night away. And then, all hell broke loose. The single scream was joined by another, and then another. Soon, a chorus of shrill screams rose from the swamps below. It could only mean one thing. The sound of running footsteps interrupted the guard's thoughts as she was joined by several colleagues, all leaning against the fence to strain for a better view. The guard ran to the nearest security terminal and punched at a button. Almost at once, the land beneath them was bathed in light. As the screeching subsided, the floodlights scanned the ground in search of the cause.

'Anything?' The guard's voice was tense as she craned forward to see.

'Nope. Nothing.' Her comrades shook their heads as they turned back from the perimeter fence. 'Probably a pack of swamp snakes.'

One by one, the searchlights were switched off and the ground below was swallowed up by darkness.

The water was still. Barely a ripple disturbed the surface. Then, as the searchlights snapped off, a small movement disturbed the water. First, Leutna Braxx appeared, his helmet breaking the surface tension. Then, his team followed. One by one, they emerged from beneath the black water. Each of them held a fistful of screech flowers by the stems. Choked of life, the plants hung limp from the troopers' hands. Keral and Boon had their helmets towards Braxx. Even through the mirrored glass of their visors, the Leutna could tell they were fuming. He couldn't allow himself another misstep or he'd risk losing his authority. Turning his thoughts back to the mission in hand, he waved his squad forward and scrambled on to the bank ahead. Waiting for their leader to join them, the troops checked their weapons for damage. Though not built to withstand long periods underwater, a quick dip had done their Heat Exchange Guns no harm. As the Leutna crouched low with his troops, he scanned the way ahead to the surveillance station. It stood incongruous against a scarlet sky, its restless antennae and radar dishes bristling in the night. The way was clear now. If they could make it through the next few hundred meters undetected, the next phase of the mission could begin. Looking round at his troops, Braxx could see they were poised for action. With a curt nod, he raised a hand to beckon them on, then took a step forward onto the muddy bank.

He felt it at once. Something impeded his progress. He didn't have to look down to know what it was. He let out a groan of disbelief. Despite all the technology at his disposal, he had been caught by the oldest trick in the book - a trip wire stretched between two metal posts hidden in the undergrowth.

'Down!' Braxx threw himself to the ground as the searchlights snapped on again. The whole area was flooded with light, exposing the Leutna and his men to the Kestran guards. A klaxon blared from the tower and Braxx's HUD flashed red in warning. 'I know!' he snapped. But there was nowhere they could go. In order to reach the relative safety of the swamp behind them, he and his troopers would have to run several metres across open ground. They'd be easy pickings. As he squinted through his visor, Braxx heard the sudden *whump* of pulse lasers. Mud and debris spattered all around him. The Kestran guards were shooting from the tower. His HUD flashing red in warning, Braxx motioned his squad to return fire. Finding what shelter they could amongst the sparse foliage, they hoisted their Heat Exchange Guns to their shoulders. As they took aim through the glare of the searchlights, the shock troops readied themselves for the kick of the HE-Guns against their bodies. At the pull of a trigger, air was drawn in through vents in the gun's barrel. It was immediately frozen via a process of heat exchange and fired at tremendous velocity towards the target in the form of ice-like bullets. The enormous heat gain was dissipated out the back of the weapon as a sheet of flame that bathed the surrounding swamp in a fiery glow. All the time, the Kestran pulse lasers found their mark. As Braxx let off a round, he heard the screams of his team. He blinked to call up the manifest once more. Each name was now displayed alongside an indication of their life signs. Within seconds, he saw three names suddenly blink red then disappear all together. Three of his team, dead. Among them, Boon. As a guard fell from the tower with a scream, Braxx switched off his HUD and directed his attention to the task at hand. Using the zoom facility on his visor, he could see the guards were being joined by others, each of them armed. The hail of laser fire increased.

'Press on!' he called to his squad. 'I'll give you cover!'

As the troops progressed towards the surveillance tower, Braxx let loose a volley of ice that strafed the observation platform above. An impact to the head sent one guard sprawling to the wall. Even in the half-light, Braxx could see the blood left on the brickwork behind them. Another clung to the perimeter fence in the last throes of life. Still the lasers criss-crossed through the night sky. Taking a moment to look at his team, Braxx saw that each of the survivors was taking a different course to the tower's ramparts. In doing so, they had lessened the chances of detection. The searchlights swept the ground in vain for the attackers. The Leutna could tell that much of the laser fire was now undirected. The guards were merely taking pot-shots in the hope of hitting someone.

At last, he was able to join his troopers at the base of the tower. They were huddled around a metal door set into the shear wall. Braxx caught his breath. Clearly the Kestrans had never considered the possibility of anyone ever making it quite this far. He and his team were now protected from fire by the curve of the tower above them. It gave them a moment of respite. He had no need for his HUD now. He could tell simply by looking just how depleted his squad now was. Of the twelve he had brought with him, just four remained. Coldly, he calculated this was still enough to make a success of the mission. He held up a hand and raised two of his fingers to indicate that the mission was continuing. Phase Two.

Three of the assembled shock troops dropped to their knees. Raising their guns to their shoulders, they flipped them round so the exhausts were now facing the door. At a signal from the Leutna, sheets of white-hot flame were directed at the door. Steam rose into the air as the metal buckled beneath the extreme heat. At last, it gave way entirely, clanging to the metal floor inside the door as it fell from its molten hinges. The shock troops lowered their weapons and made way for the last of their number. Keral stepped forward, unbuckling a light grenade from her belt. Peering in through the hatch, she could see the shadows of the advancing guards. Pulling a pin on her grenade, she lobbed it into the corridor beyond. Within moments, a flash of brilliant white light filled the space. The guards' shadows flashed sharp against the walls. As the Kestrans fell back, shielding their eyes against the intense glare, Keral pulled another grenade from her belt. Just as the guards drew their weapons to fight back, they were enveloped by a cloud of noxious blue gas as Keral's smoke grenade arced through the air to land at their feet. The shock troops' visors cut through the fog, picking out the guards' silhouettes in red. One by one, the three remaining troopers cut them down with a hail of ice bullets. Leutna Braxx urged his depleted squad forwards, shooting from the hip as he did so. More light grenades whistled above his head as a platoon of Kestran guards filled the corridor, their pulse lasers criss-crossing in the air. Explosions flashed ahead of him, the blue smoke shielding him from the guards' guns. A prolonged burst from his HE-Gun sent his opponents reeling. Some clutched at their chests where the ice bullets had found a home, others buckled as their legs were cut away from beneath them. Braxx allowed himself a smile. This was too easy. Soon, they had made progress through the corridor to a curved wall. Waving two of his team on, he crouched by the door with Keral. She nodded her head in readiness.

Giving the other two men time to get to their positions, the Leutna reached down to his utility belt. Retrieving a sonic explosive unit from a pouch, he attached it to the door. Knowing a fellow trooper would be doing exactly the same thing to a door just out of sight, he set the device to couple with its partner down the corridor. It flashed to show it had connected. Braxx knew he wouldn't even have to shield his eyes. The blast would be concentrated into the metal of the door, shaking it from its hinges and disabling the lock mechanism. Sure enough, after emitting a high-pitched bleep, the device transmitted a violent sonic shock to the metal. The door blew inwards. Keral threw a smoke grenade after it as Braxx stepped through the aperture, his HE gun blazing. Ice bullets ricocheted from the walls in a cacophony of sound. Kestran operatives threw themselves to the floor behind their consoles in panic. A small group of guards rose from a table, one to punch at a button on the wall marked '*Emergency*', the others to reach for their laser rifles. But they were too late. Two other shock troops had smashed their way in through the door behind them. Taken by surprise, the guards had no time to turn before they were cut down, their blood splattering on the playing cards they had discarded on the table. Steel shutters began to descend over the windows in the curved walls. The guards defeated, the operatives lunged for their guns to return fire. The four Zargons were merciless. Standing firm, they raked the room with ice. Soon, the battle was over. The operatives were outgunned and, frankly, outclassed. Braxx stood with his team in the silence then lunged to a console and stabbed at a button. With a whirring of hidden fans, the smoke in the room began to dissipate. The Leutna surveyed the scene. Looking across the room at his two colleagues, he motioned to a far console with his gun.

'Do it!' he barked over his comms.

The troopers sprang to a smoking panel that bristled with instrumentation and smashed it with the butts of their guns. Reaching down, one of them wrenched a panel from its position, sparks flying to the floor. Looking about him to see that they had missed nothing, Leutna Braxx ordered his squad from the room and pulled a light grenade from his belt. Cycling through the options with a finger, he selected 'blast' and pulled the pin. One last glance to see the room was clear and Braxx let go the grenade. Seeing it lodge in a burned out console near the centre of the room, Braxx grunted in satisfaction then followed his team out of the room to the corridor beyond.

For a while, the room was silent. Then, movement. An operative, stunned from the fight, was pulling himself from the floor. Grabbing at a chair, he heaved his top half onto a console, gasping for breath. Blood ran from a deep wound in his head. Wiping sweat from his eyes, he tried to focus on the object before him. A small round device that seemed wedged in the circuitry. Just as he started to make sense of the scene before him, the grenade glowed a vicious red and exploded into a ball of fire.

The troop carrier rose into the air, vertical thrusters illuminating the ground below. The pilot had no need to be so careful now, and so the vehicle banked alarmingly before climbing. He punched a button on the control console and the blast shields slid up to reveal windows along the vehicle's sides and the entire length of the roof. Craning forward, the Leutna just had time to see the surveillance tower consumed by a fireball before the craft punched through the cloud. Adjusting his visor to cut though the cloud layer, he watched as the tower crumbled in on itself and toppled to the swampy ground. He looked around the hold at the remainder of his squad. Keral sat directly opposite, her visor up, breathing heavily. The trooper next to her nursed a bruised arm. Braxx met Keral's gaze. Just as he was wondering how to react to her, the cabin shook. Buffeted by the last remnants of atmospheric turbulence, the craft slid into the enormity of space. Braxx felt the ship tilt as it altered course.

There, ahead of them, hung the vast bulk of the Zargon battle cruiser. As the craft approached, the cruiser looked huge in comparison. Soon, it was all Braxx could see through the window. Alerted to their approach, a bay door was opening in its hull. The carrier oriented itself to the cruiser's position. Braxx felt the engines cut out. The pilot was relying on their own momentum now. Skilfully, he guided the craft into the bay and onto the rails that projected from the floor. Engaging the clamps, he sat back with a look of satisfaction on his face. Slowly, the vehicle was pulled into the bowels of the cruiser. As Braxx looked up through the window in the carrier's roof, he could see the cavernous interior extending above him for what seemed miles. There, held by gantries in the very centre of the bay, hung the huge barrel of the Interplanetary Ballistic Missile Launcher. Even at this distance, it was a fearsome sight. Its surface seemed to ripple with a barely contained energy. The bay door closed behind them and the craft nestled into its place by an interior shutter. Braxx took a breath as he reached to release his restraints. He wasn't looking forward to the debrief.

With a brilliant flare of its thrusters and an almost deafening crack, the battle cruiser accelerated away. In no time at all, it became nothing more than just another speck in the vastness of the universe.

II

PREDATOR AND PREY

The needle-like minarets of Estoran glistened beneath Kestra's five moons. It had been the planet's capital since it had united under one government many centuries before. The President's official residence had been built at the city's very heart. Its yellow brick perimeter walls encircled lush gardens and graceful temples. Pools of bright blue water shimmered beneath the stars and fronds of exotic trees wafted in the breeze.

Inside, the furnishing and decor was impressive but informal. Discreet lighting and unusually designed fountains gave a feeling of tranquillity quite at odds with the President's tense facade. He paced among the plush furniture in agitation, his noble brow creased into a furrow of concern. He had the slender physique of all his race, but there was something powerful about him, too. Before him, at a large reflective table, sat his chief intelligence advisor and a colonel from the intelligence corps.

'So, we're blind on the southern approaches?' The President spoke softly but with authority. He stopped mid-stride to watch for the Colonel's reaction. She sat, tidily, with her hands clasped before her. Her silver uniform and shining gold epaulettes spoke of someone for whom presentation was everything. She stared thoughtfully out the window for a moment, then turned her almond eyes upon the President.

'Unfortunately, Mr President, the situation is far worse.' She gave the President a moment to absorb the news. 'The raiding party took with them the DS24 scanner.'

The President raised his eyebrows. 'Explain, Captain Thawn.'

The Intelligence Captain took up the baton to continue. 'Meaning they have all the information they need to jam our other stations.'

The Colonel nodded. 'The ship was positively identified. It was Zargon.'

The President sighed as he took a seat at the table and ran his fingers through his mane of jet-black hair. 'Then we must expect an attack?'

Thawn nodded. 'I'm afraid, Mr President, that has to be the conclusion.' He lowered his voice, ominously. 'It means war.'

The President allowed his breath to whistle out through his teeth. 'A war we cannot win, and one we cannot afford to lose.'

Above the planet's surface, a very old, very battered freighter moved through space. It seemed to require a great deal of effort, its huge aft engines moaning in complaint. Even in the vacuum of the void, it was possible to imagine the sound of rattling coming from the hull plates. An old, reliable workhorse from a different age, the B156 Transporter bore the distinctive hammerhead design of the original fleet. In the cockpit, lounging back in the astro-pilot's seat, his feet on the flight dash, sat John Lovell. An Earthman who admitted to being around forty years of age, Lovell spent much of his time travelling round the galaxy, ferrying anything to anyone if the price was right. He rubbed his lantern jaw as he spoke, his voice a lazy drawl.

'Move around,' he was saying. 'Stay loose. Life gets serious soon enough.'

'That's your considered advice to the young?' came a voice from beside him.

Lovell considered for a moment. 'Sure,' he said at last, though he didn't sound so sure.

Lovell glanced across the cockpit to the seat opposite. Clarence B. Bond sat at the controls. He was everything Lovell could wish for in a co-pilot, particularly if he wished for a talking chimpanzee. There were times when Lovell had reason to curse the enormous advances made in animal psychology, particularly when Clarence answered back, argued or had been proven right again. Once the larger Earth primates had broken through the speech barrier, there was no stopping them. A third generation emancipated ape and proud of it, Clarence B. Bond was sophisticated, intelligent and articulate. And boy, didn't Lovell know it.

'I disagree,' replied Clarence, with more than a note of smugness in his voice. Lovell readied himself for the inevitable onslaught of well-argued prose. 'I consider the advantages of a good education should be instilled in the youth, as early as possible.'

Lovell rolled his eyes. 'With a Masters degree in astronautics, what else are you going to say?'

Clarence straightened his smart, white tunic. As immaculately cut as it was, the chimp was fooling no one. Lovell knew there was a hell of a lot of fur under there. 'Astrophysics, actually.'

'And where did that get you?' Lovell snorted. 'Bumming around the galaxy! Hitching a ride with me.' He leaned even further back in his seat so it looked in danger of snapping right off.

Clarence sniffed his disapproval. 'I happen to be on vacation.'

'Vacation?'

'From the Institute of Advanced Military Philosophy,' the chimp nodded, haughtily.

Lovell stared at him. 'The deal was that you *worked* your passage.' He swung his feet from the dash and his seat sprang upright. 'Take over!' he growled. Rising to his feet with a groan, Lovell headed for the ship's interior, muttering under his breath. 'Vacation? He thinks he's on vacation…'

'Er, I think we've got company.'

The note of caution in Clarence's voice brought Lovell to a halt. Turning on his heels, he leaned over his co-pilot's shoulder to look at a monitor. A trace was moving across the screen.

'Closing fast.' Clarence jabbed a finger at the blip as it neared the centre.

'Let's take a look,' breathed Lovell, suddenly worried. 'Hit visual.'

Clarence punched a control button and the ship's main viewer crackled before them. Lovell squinted into the static. 'I'm not seeing anything, Clarence.'

Clarence sighed. The viewer was a relic from a bygone age. Like Lovell himself, it sometimes needed a little coaxing. The chimp hit the side of the panel hard with the flat of his hairy hand. Slowly, the picture cleared and three shapes started to coalesce through the noise.

'Kestran Interceptors,' hissed Lovell, his concern growing.

The three craft were flying in close formation, their sleek lines seeming to accentuate their speed. Lovell ducked as they flashed past. He immediately felt foolish.

'What the hell?' he hissed to hide his embarrassment. 'Tell those jokers to cool it.'

Pretending not to have noticed, Clarence leaned into the radio. 'We are an Earth registered Transporter,' he announced, his voice calm.

'Tell them we're unarmed,' Lovell interrupted, his panic rising.

' – and we are not armed,' the chimp concluded, pointedly.

Clearly having not heard or chosen to ignore Clarence's declaration, the three interceptors banked round for another run.

'They're coming again.' Clarence noticed Lovell gripping the dash. His knuckles were white.

The two pilots watched as the three craft banked, their engines blazing. *They're certainly nimble*, thought Lovell, *I'll give 'em that. Which means we don't stand a chance.* Their speed increasing, the interceptors buzzed the freighter again. Lovell was sure he could feel his ship being rocked in their slipstream.

'They come any closer,' offered Clarence, breezily, 'and we could shake their hands hello.'

Lovell blinked the sweat from his eyes. 'Let me talk to them.'

Clarence looked at his companion for a moment, weighing up his likely actions. Lovell looked worried. Perhaps it was best to allow him the illusion of being in control for a moment. With a curt nod, the chimpanzee slid from his seat, his knuckles dragging against the floor as he made room.

Lovell punched the radio on. 'You listen to me you suicide jockeys – '

Clarence rolled his eyes. That sort of approach was bound to work.

'YOU ARE VIOLATING KESTRAN RESTRICTED SPACE.'

Lovell's hands went to his ears as he winced in pain.

'Woh!' Clarence stabbed at the controls. 'You really need to fix that volume switch.'

'I repeat,' came the voice again, quieter now. 'You are violating restricted space.'

Clarence's fingers were dancing across the controls. Lovell was keenly aware of just how agile he could be when he wanted. 'I have to agree,' said the ape, at last, pointing to a chart. 'We're within the million mile limit.'

Lovell grimaced. Why did Clarence always have to be right? 'Listen, friend,' he began, leaning back into the radio, 'I'm having a little trouble here with the navigation computer.'

Clarence nodded, obligingly. 'That true,' he concurred. 'It's obsolete.'

Lovell glared at him, then turned his attention back to the comms panel. 'We'll just alter course and get out your hair, okay?'

There was a brief pause, then a crackle of static. 'Follow us.' Then the channel went dead. There was clearly no discussion to be had. Looking up at the view screen, Lovell could see the three interceptors had formed a close formation around his freighter. His eyes flickered furtively as he turned back to Clarence.

'When I say go, swing to port and give her full thrust,' he whispered.

'I don't know why you're whispering,' said Clarence in response. 'Comms are off.'

'Just do it!' Lovell barked in exasperation.

'Are you proposing we try and outrun them?' Clarence's eyes swivelled comically around the cockpit. 'In this?'

'Why should they chase us?' Lovell shrugged. 'So, we're a few miles off course. Where's the big problem?' Clarence stared back. It was one of those moments, thought Lovell, where he'd have to assert his dominance. 'Listen,' he began, raising his voice in what he hoped was a show of authority, 'I'm in charge of this ship - '

'Then you'll accept complete responsibility?' soothed Clarence. This was an old game and he knew how to play it.

Lovell nodded. 'Yes.' There was a pause as the chimpanzee held him in his gaze. 'What?' he gasped. 'You want it in writing?'

Clarence narrowed his eyes. 'Wouldn't want to tax you too much.' Resigned, he hauled himself back into his seat and nudged at the controls.

'Go!'

Clarence hit the thruster and the freighter swung immediately to port, accelerating away. Lovell kept his eyes nervously on the screen as the interceptors followed.

'They're still with us,' said Clarence, redundantly.

Lovell took a breath. 'Keep going.'

Clarence leaned his weight against the throttle as the cockpit began to rattle in protest. Somewhere from behind, he heard something falling over.

'Hold on!'

Lovell's tone caused Clarence to look back up at the screen. A missile was streaking from the lead interceptor. Glancing at a monitor on the dash, the chimp could see its intended target was the freighter's port engine. 'It'll cripple us,' he said, simply.

Before Clarence had a chance to change course, the missile exploded just off the freighter's bow. Lovell gripped the console again as the ship was buffeted by the blast.

'Just a warning shot.'

The comms sprang to life with a burst of static. 'Alter course!' It was the interceptor pilot again. 'This is your final warning.'

'Bluff,' Lovell smirked. 'They wouldn't dare hit a neutral ship.'

'Er, Lovell?'

Lovell looked to his companion. Clarence was pointing to the screen. Another missile was streaking through the blackness of space. They both followed its course as it passed behind the freighter. A pause. Then a bang. The ship rocked on the wave of the explosion, more extreme than before. Flung from the control dash by the force of the blast, Lovell found himself flailing to grab anything to hold onto.

'What are those maniacs doing?'

Clarence was scanning the instrumentation in front of him, a picture of calm. 'Well, it looks like they've just blown a hole in the side of number three hold.' He turned to Lovell. 'Just a warning shot,' he added, sarcastically.

III

ARRIVAL

Now under escort, the freighter swung through the lower atmosphere to land at the largest of Kestra's space ports. Thrusters hissing, it heaved itself onto the landing pad with an audible crunch. As the engines powered down, it was clear to see that one of them had been damaged. A great gash caused by the missile explosion seeped steam and gases into the Kestran air. Their work done, the three interceptors banked away and on to their next rendezvous.

From a small cluster of buildings beneath a monorail terminus, a telescopic walkway unfolded itself and reached towards Lovell's freighter. Connecting with a portal in the craft's hull, it magnetized itself to the metal plates.

Inside, Lovell and Clarence waited by the airlock.

'I'll sue them,' muttered Lovell, darkly. 'I'll sue them for the entire value of the ship.'

'That much?' replied Clarence, feigning interest. Resting his knuckles on the floor, he looked up at the freighter pilot. He didn't think he'd ever seen Lovell look so hangdog.

The airlock door slid open with a hiss and the two pilots stepped through. In the walkway, stood three uniformed guards, their laser guns drawn. They both had the distinctive almond shaped eyes of the Kestran race. One of them, the tallest, stepped forward.

'Name?' he rasped.

'John Lovell. And I want to see someone in authority. NOW!' Lovell was seething.

The guard held out a hand to placate him. 'You will.' He turned to his colleagues. 'Take him for interrogation.'

Before Lovell could react, the guards had caught him by the arms and proceeded to lead him off down the walkway. The taller guard waited until Lovell had rounded a corner with his captors before turning to the chimpanzee.

'You must be - ', he began.

'Clarence B. Bond,' the chimp confirmed cheerfully. Peering through the guard's helmet visor, he could he was smiling.

'Welcome to Kestra.'

Lovell was despondent. As he sat between the two guards inside the monorail carriage, he let his eyes wander down to the landing pad below. The sight of the gaping wound in his freighter's engine did little to lift his spirits.

'Where are we going?' he asked as he felt a sudden jolt of speed. The scene below slipped away to be replaced by the darkness of a tunnel interior. Neither of his guards offered an answer. Instead they sat, impassive, their guns trained at his chest.

Lovell tried a different tack. 'Either of you heard the one about the girl and the astronaut who got stuck in a time warp?' He leaned back in his seat. The guards stared back, stone-faced. 'Hey, did you hear me?' In response, one of the guards levelled his gun at his midriff. Lovell smiled weakly and leaned back again.

Suddenly, they were through the tunnel. The monorail system provided the perfect views of Kestra's landscape. The morning light glanced off the mountain tops, flooding the valley with light. Tall towers pierced the sky, their yellow brick warming in the sun. It was a picture of peace.

The train slowed as it reached the city. Looking through the window, Lovell could see the terminal nestling in a large complex of buildings. Built of glass and stone, the air about them shimmered in a haze of heat. If he had been in a different frame of mind entirely, Lovell had no doubt he would have enjoyed the journey. As it was, he allowed himself to be hauled to his feet by the guards and led through the train door into a long corridor. Squinting into the bright lights positioned overhead, he was marshalled along the corridor, his footsteps echoing off the smooth walls. The guards flanked him at every turn to prevent his escape. Eventually, a doorway slid open to admit access to a large, tastefully furnished room. Pushed inside by the muzzle of a laser gun, Lovell took in his surroundings. Concealed lighting gave the room a warm, intimate feel in spite of its size. A central, sculptured rock pool was surrounded by a number of exotic plants. Seating areas were dotted around the room with small tables in between. A couple of loungers were positioned by the pool. Just as he turned to question his guards, Lovell heard the hiss of a closing door and realised they had gone.

Colonel Zana wasn't particularly impressed with what she saw. Her almond eyes narrowed as she gazed through the dome of one-way glass set into the floor of the observation room. Beneath it, she could see Lovell pacing the room below. The only time he stopped, Zana noticed, was to admire and preen himself in one of the decorative mirrors set into the walls. The colonel cast her eyes at the Intelligence Captain to her right and rolled her eyes. The Captain allowed himself a smile as he tore a readout from a computer terminal.

'Psychic scan positive,' Thawn drawled.

'What's in his file?'

The Captain leaned forward to stab at a button and focus on a monitor. 'John D. Lovell,' he read. 'Served in Earth Star Fleet, captained Space Fighter. Active service in war with Centaurians. Decorated for bravery.' He raised an eyebrow in surprise, then looked through the glass dome to the room below. Colonel Zana smiled. It was as if he were trying to marry the evidence of his own eyes with the readout on the monitor. She had to admit she'd had the same thought. For all that she could see, Lovell was a shambling figure in badly fitting pants. 'Commended by the Galactic Federation,' concluded the Captain, 'for outstanding service.'

Zana shrugged. What did she know, after all? 'I suppose... he *could* be suitable.'

Captain Thawn punched a button to scroll the text forward and read on. 'Resigned commission.'

'Any reason?' Zana frowned.

'None given.'

The Colonel stroked her chin as she thought. 'Go on.'

Thawn peered into the monitor again. 'Started small shipping business, bought an ex-Federation B156 Transporter, had a contract to ship tricanium ore.' He shook his head.

'Expired,' came a voice from behind them.

Zana spun round to acknowledge the interjection. 'Thank you, Mr Bond.'

There, feeling more comfortable than he had in a long while, sat Clarence B. Bond, his squat frame sprawled on a lounger. He winked mischievously at Zana as he pulled the ring on a can of beer.

'Anything else, Captain?' The Colonel turned her attention back to the figure below.

'Just physical details.'

Colonel Zana nodded. 'Have everything transcribed and on my desk by the morning.'

Captain Thawn snapped to attention as Zana moved to the door, casting a final look at the ape in the chair as she passed. Clarence let go a beery belch in response and held up a hand in apology. 'Pardon me,' he smiled.

'Captain Lovell.'

Lovell was embarrassed at having been caught looking at himself in the mirror but, frankly, there had been little else to do. Besides, he was a handsome devil and sometimes he just couldn't help himself. Turning swiftly on his heels, he was met by the tall, slim figure of Colonel Zana stepping through the door. Lovell tried to hide the fact that his pupils had involuntarily dilated.

'Just plain John these days,' he said, breezily, his eye falling on the epaulettes on her shoulder. 'Colonel.'

The door sliding shut behind her, Zana walked to a section of the wall that was marked by a small depression in the plasterwork. 'Can I offer you a drink? Faras or juda, perhaps?' She turned, awaiting his response.

'Er, I'll take a beer, thanks.'

'Sorry, no beer. Coffee?'

Lovell sighed. 'That'll be fine.'

Colonel Zana turned back to the wall. 'Coffee for one,' she commanded to nothing in particular. Who she was talking to, Lovell had no idea. The order placed, Zana walked to the water feature in the middle of the room, her hands trailing absently among the fronds of the exotic plants. 'I have a problem,' she began. 'I wonder if you can help me?'

Lovell hooked his thumbs in his belt loops and puffed out his chest. For some reason, he felt eager to impress. 'Be glad to, if I can.'

Their conversation was interrupted by a soft beeping from the wall, and Lovell turned to see a panel sliding aside to reveal a cup of coffee. His eyes grew wide. 'Well, I'll be,' he grinned.

Zana moved briskly to hand the cup to her captive and the wall unit hummed closed again. The Colonel took a seat on the rocks by the fountain. 'First I must apologise for the damage to your ship. Our pilots are a little nervous at present.'

Lovell blew out his cheeks. 'I'll say.'

'We will, of course, carry out the necessary repairs.'

Seizing the opportunity to get closer to the Colonel, Lovell squeezed onto the rock next to her, sipping from his coffee. 'These things happen,' he began, magnanimously. He winced as he took a sip of his coffee, barely able to conceal that it tasted like ink. 'You said you needed help?' he continued, as much to distract himself from the taste than anything else.

Zana lowered her eyes, running her fingers over a small bell-like flower. To Lovell's wonderment, it tinkled deliciously. Her next phrase filled the captain with a cruel hope. 'You could be just the man I'm looking for.'

With that, Colonel Zana turned to walk away, beckoning him to follow with a flash of her almond eyes. As the doorway slid open and Zana stepped through to the corridor beyond, Lovell tipped the dregs of his coffee into one of the pot plants by the fountain. He was surprised to hear the plant give a grunt of disapproval, and he was sure he noticed the petals flinch in shock.

IV

A PROPOSITION

The sun blazed out from the centre of the solar system. On each side of the boiling star and roughly equidistant from it, two planets processed gracefully in their orbits. Around one, could be seen the five distinctive Kestran moons.

'Here is our planet.'

The Colonel had led Lovell down an unremarkable corridor, much like the one that had led him to the previous room where he had been held. In fact, it might very well have been the exact same corridor, but Lovell couldn't be sure. He hadn't yet been given the opportunity to get his bearings.

Zana was pointing at the image that hung before them, indicating Kestra and her five celestial companions. Making sure she had Lovell's attention, the Colonel walked around the image and pointed to the planet on the other side of the sun. 'And here is Zargon.'

Lovell nodded eagerly. He was trying desperately to appear interested but, in truth, he had no idea where this was heading. And he was still struggling with the acrid taste of the coffee at the back of his throat. 'That's great, but can we get something to eat?' He winked, lasciviously. 'Maybe a drink?'

'Last night,' continued Zana, seemingly oblivious to his appeals, 'a Zargon strike force knocked out one of our surveillance stations.'

Seeing he was getting nowhere with his requests, Lovell turned reluctantly to the three dimensional display before him. Stepping back to take in the scale of the model, something struck him. 'Long way to come for a hit and run job,' he breathed.

'They didn't come from Zargon,' replied Zana, simply. 'We think the attack was mounted from here.' She held up a clenched hand, then spread her fingers wide to zoom in on the image before them. A small, spinning rock came into view on the Kestran side of the sun. 'An uninhabited asteroid,' she said, pointedly. With a wave of her hand, the display blinked off and the lights in the room snapped up. For the first time, Lovell looked around him. The room was bare except for a large table that sat in the centre of the floor. 'Or at least, we thought it uninhabited until we saw this.'

Striding to the table, Zana flipped open a concealed control panel in its side and stabbed at a button. Suddenly, the whole table top was illuminated with a high definition image of the surface of the asteroid. Leaning forward, Lovell could see heavy equipment moving about a huge excavation sight.

'Is this live?' he asked.

Zana shook her head. 'This is footage from three months ago.'

Guessing it worked on the same principle as the three dimensional image he had just been shown, Lovell reached out his hand and spread his fingers to zoom in. The dig site had been gouged into the top of a huge column of rock. 'Must be two thousand feet tall,' he whistled. He noticed Zana said nothing to contradict him. 'That is one large hole. Who made it?'

'The Zargon forces.'

Lovell raised an eyebrow 'The people who raided you last night?'

Zana nodded. 'They own the asteroid.'

Lovell peered down to the table top image. Even as he watched, he could see the excavation taking place. Great hulks of machinery carried boulders of rock from the escarpment. Excavators cut into the rock. Intermittent explosions made headway into the more troublesome seams.

'They said it was a geological survey,' explained Zana.

Lovell scoffed at the idea. 'The last geologist I saw had a half pound hammer and a micro seismograph.'

Colonel Zana waved her hand over the table. A series of images flashed past. Lovell could tell they were archive pictures and, as the sequence continued, they told the story of the excavation's development and enlargement. First, the hole was blasted into the column of rock, then machinery was introduced to deepen it further still. Soon, a complex interior was being constructed. Tunnels were dug into the rock surface and platforms were created at intermediate points.

'A month ago,' Zana explained, 'the structure was finished.' The table top had gone blank. Lovell waited for the next image. 'No picture?'

In reply to Lovell's question, Zana pressed another control on the console. Quite unexpectedly, the table top slid away to show a scale model of the completed construction. Lovell's mouth hung open in surprise. It looked like a walled fortress had been created on top of the column of rock.

'The scale is a thousand to one,' said Zana. 'Gives you some idea of the size.' She smiled to herself. She had certainly got his attention now. She could hear him mumbling to himself as he walked around the table, studying the details of the model intently.

'Defensive lasers, launch pads, fighters.' Lovell scratched at the stubble on his chin.

'How many men?' Zana asked.

Lovell shrugged then leaned on the table top to get a better view. 'To man a place like this? Two, three thousand.' He noticed the Colonel flinch.

'What kind of strike power?' she asked, hesitantly.

'Impossible to even guess.'

Colonel Zana folded her arms and leaned against the table. 'Our estimate is up to ten battle cruisers armed with Interplanetary Ballistic Missiles.' She met Lovell's gaze. 'Four could obliterate this planet,' the Colonel concluded.

Lovell had to be honest; his heart had skipped a beat at the news. He turned back to the model. 'A jump-off point for an all out assault.'

Zana was trying hard not to look frightened. 'A loaded gun aimed at the head of every single person on Kestra,' she said, sadly.

Lovell was silent. Suddenly, the model fortress looked more ominous and even more formidable. A thought occurred to him. There must be a reason for his involvement. He turned to Colonel Zana, his thumbs in his belt loops. 'Why show me all this?'

Zana dropped her hands and took a step towards him, locking him in her gaze. 'We want you to destroy that fortress,' she said, simply.

Lovell was stunned into silence.

'More coffee?' There was a glint of mischief in the Colonel's almond eyes.

Lovell frowned, his thoughts suddenly chaotic. 'You're not serious?'

'Why?' replied Zana, suddenly playful. 'Did it taste that bad?'

Clarence B. Bond lay sprawled on a couch. A screen embedded in the wall was playing his favourite movie. A table next to him was littered with the remnants of a meal. Some crumbs of cheese, a few grapes and the remains of some maize based snack were all that was left on his plate. A couple of empty beer cans rolled at his feet. Despite his relaxed demeanour, his white tunic was as pristine as ever. The chimpanzee tore his eyes away from the screen as the door slid open.

Lovell took a step into the room, looking more dishevelled than ever. His hair was tousled and his brow furrowed. 'How they treating you?' he asked, seeing Clarence before him.

'Fine,' Clarence admitted. 'The beer's great.'

'Huh?' Lovell huffed. 'I was told there *was* no beer.'

Clarence shrugged. 'I guess I asked nicely,' he said. 'Screen off.'

The movie screen went blank at his command and the concealed lighting in the ceiling flickered into life. Looking around him, Lovell could see he had found himself in some sort of recreation facility. Shelves of books and magazines lined the walls in a library corner. Three dimensional holographic games stood waiting for players in another, their welcome screens revolving in mid air. In another corner, Lovell saw some old-fashioned table top games and, against a far wall, a jukebox. Clearly, Clarence had been enjoying a very different form of Kestran greeting.

'And you?' asked the ape, trying to sound as concerned as possible.

Lovell threw himself onto a chair by some exotic pot plants. 'These people are weird,' he hissed as he ran his fingers through his hair in exasperation. 'D'you know what they want me to do?'

Clarence decided to humour him. 'What's that?'

Lovell thought for a moment. 'Ah, forget it. It's crazy.' Suddenly agitated, he ran back to the doorway, trying in vain to open it. There wasn't even any sign of a handle. 'How d'you open this damn thing?'

Clarence reached for the last of his meal as he spoke, his agile fingers probing a tube of Shnibble Snacks. 'You don't.'

Lovell spun round, his eyes wide in fury. 'We're locked in?'

'You're under indictment,' Clarence shrugged as he smacked the salt from his lips.

'For what?' Lovell was clearly incensed. Clarence could see him grinding his teeth, a sure sign that he was about to blow.

None too helpfully, the chimp held up his fingers to count off the charges one by one. 'Violating restricted space. Disregarding those Interceptors. And your ship isn't space worthy.'

Strangely, it was this last charge that seemed to hurt Lovell the most. 'Technicalities,' he said as he waved them away.

'You could get two years,' warned Clarence as he reached for another beer. To be honest, he was eager to get back to the movie. He hadn't seen it in some time and had forgotten how it ended.

Lovell crashed back onto the chair, a look of defeat clouding his grizzled features. 'Two years?'

Clarence nodded. 'Unless of course - '

Lovell rolled his eyes. Here it comes, he thought. 'Unless of course *what?*'

The chimp shrugged innocently as if the whole affair was nothing to do with him.

'What?' demanded Lovell as he strode over to him. 'I want to know.'

'Unless of course,' began Clarence again, as if he were explaining the situation to a child, 'you were to consider accepting the mission.'

The silence was thick enough to cut with a knife. Lovell blinked furiously as he fought to think through the implications of the chimp's remarks. So, Clarence was involved all along. Lovell lifted a finger to stab at the chimp as he retorted. 'You can tell your pals I'll take the two years.'

'You really think this man is our best hope to lead the attack?'

The President let Zana's report fall to the desk. Through one of the large windows that lined his room, he could see the horizon streaked with scarlet, the beautiful dawning of another day. The collection of private rooms was infused with the scent of exotic plants. Almost everywhere Zana looked, there was an abundance of colourful foliage. She knew that almost every home on Kestra was the same, but the President's private residence was famed for its collection of native flora. Carved in the rock face of Estoran's highest mountain, the palace was a beacon of magnificence.

The President had called this working breakfast in light of Zana's meeting with Lovell. Bowls of soft fruit were scattered around the table alongside plates of bread and sweet cakes.

Jugs of a pink coloured liquid stood, half empty, amongst the detritus of a finished meal. The President dabbed his lips with a napkin and looked at Zana, eager to hear her response. To his right, Captain Thawn downed the dregs of juice from a strangely curved glass and sat back in his chair in anticipation.

Her breakfast done, Zana lay her spoon to one side. 'I admit, he's by no means ideal.' She thought she detected a snort of derision from Thawn. Regardless, she ploughed on. 'But the one great advantage is that he's an Earthman. A neutral.'

The President nodded in thought, aware of the wave of cynicism coming from the man at his right elbow. 'I see,' he began. 'If the plan failed, we'd have to deny any complicity.' He turned to the Intelligence Captain. 'What are our chances?'

'Slim,' the man barked back at once. It was as if he had been waiting for his moment to denounce the whole scheme. 'With a little luck, a *specialised* group might just pull it off.' He looked pointedly at Zana. 'Lovell is far from specialised.'

'He's better than that,' smiled Zana. 'He's expendable. And deniable. He gets caught, we wash our hands of the whole affair.'

'It seems a little...' the President searched for the right word. 'Underhand,' he said at last.

'Needs must, sir,' Zana retorted, a note of steel in her voice.

There was a silence as the President weighed up the options, his slim fingers drumming on the table top.

'The fortress is virtually impregnable,' snapped Captain Thawn at last, eager to sway his President away from what he regarded as a hopeless mission. 'It's a fool's errand.'

'Then perhaps,' sighed the President at last, 'John D. Lovell is just the man.'

V

THE FACE OF THE ENEMY

The asteroid's surface was rugged, rocky and inhospitable. Its grey, monotone landscape was marked with sheer escarpments and unyielding peaks. Fissures riddled the surface like scars. As it spun slowly through the blackness of space, it was the picture of desolation, bleak and forbidding.

From the top of a column of rock, came the unmistakable sound of Heat Exchange gunfire, echoing across the plain beneath. From the rim came a body, arcing through the air, twisting lifelessly as it fell. It bounced sickeningly off the rock face several times before finally crashing onto the rocks below. There it settled amongst the other corpses and bones, the grisly remains of previous executions.

Two thousand feet above the plain, the fortress nestled on top of the column of rock. Considering the rock face was completely unscalable, the concrete perimeter wall seemed almost redundant. Angled at forty-five degrees, it jutted out over the surrounding precipice and was, itself, over a hundred feet in height. Set into concrete blocks and placed at intervals around the wall, High Energy Laser Cannons pointed skyward. In the enclosed space beyond them, space fighters squatted on launch pads surrounded by fuel tanks and military buildings bristling with antennae.

On the wall itself, another Zargon soldier stood, trembling, trying not to look at the drop behind him. His hands were tied behind his back. As he stood quivering on the parapet, the six-man execution squad in front of him raised their HE-Guns.

The officer barked a command, and the soldiers fired. There was a blaze of heat from the HE-Guns' rear and every shot hit its mark. The soldier was sent reeling over the wall's edge to join his comrades in death below.

Almost at once, another soldier was manhandled into the same spot. His legs buckling beneath him, he fought the urge to retch as he contemplated his fate. As the soldier was propped against a buttress to hold him up, the officer in charge broke ranks to stride across the wall to Grand Leutna Gahn. Gahn was an imposing figure, his face seemingly chiselled from the rock of the benighted asteroid below. His eyes were cold as space itself. The officer couldn't help but shiver as he approached his superior.

'This is the last of them, sir. For now.' He swallowed beneath the unbending gaze of the Grand Leutna. 'Jol Lenda, late for guard duty.'

Grand Leutna Gahn nodded, disinterestedly. He'd never heard of the man. He dare say he wouldn't be missed. Anyway, this was quicker than any court martial. Gahn gestured to the officer with an impatient wave of his baton and the subordinate nodded to his men. Another blast of HE gunfire saw the condemned man twisting into the air and over the precipice.

Below them, as the unfortunate soldier began his descent to the rocks below, there came the sudden, deep rumble of heavy gears. An immense section of the rock face, some six hundred feet across and three hundred feet high, began to open. Pivoting at the base, it slowly lowered to provide a platform. Within, in an enormous area hewn out of the solid rock, six huge Space Battle Cruisers. Even at their enormous size, they were dwarfed by the interior cavern. Gantries lined the walls. Holes punched into the rock face led to a warren of dimly lit corridors and access passages. Operatives sat at computer consoles, technicians busied themselves at heavy machinery and, everywhere, soldiers stood guard. The air in the cavern shimmered as a Space Battle Cruiser began its journey to the mouth of the hangar. After seeming to rest a moment, there was a roar of engines. With a mighty effort, the huge craft lifted vertically off the ramp and into the black void above. The grinding of machinery could be heard again as the rocky platform began to close.

Having left the execution squad to their work, the Grand Leutna stood overlooking the hangar to watch the vehicle's launch. The Battle Cruiser gone, the shaft of daylight from the entrance narrowed and finally disappeared. Grand Leutna Gahn turned from the window and resumed his progress through the corridor. Hewn from solid rock, the walls around him glistened in the artificial light. Here and there, a mineral seam could be raced in the walls before disappearing into the rock face. At intervals, thick steel doors opened to admit groups of Zargon guards. They snapped to attention and saluted as the Grand Leutna passed by. He enjoyed the looks of fear in their eyes. Nodding to two sentries either side of the corridor, Gahn approached a heavy airlock. It swung open to admit him and the Grand Leutna found himself in the central computer room.

The natural rock of the walls had been painted silver and the floor was smooth and polished. Banks of computers lined the walls, their flashing lights bouncing off the silver paintwork. Gahn walked to a table in the centre of the room. There stood Leutna Braxx, standing respectfully to attention. Gahn resisted telling him to stand at ease. He loved playing these games.

'Well?' he barked.

Leutna Braxx swallowed. 'We have broken the coding and computed the frequencies.'

Grand Leutna Gahn glanced down to the table. He recognised the DS24 scanner that Braxx and his squad had taken from the Kestran Electronic Surveillance Station. It had been connected up to the surrounding computer banks via several cables. It seemed to pulsate with power. Periodically, it would emit a series of electronic bleeps. Two Zargon technicians, their eyes cast down for fear of meeting the Grand Leutna's gaze, busied themselves interpreting the readouts.

'We can blind the Kestran's electronic eyes. They'll never see us coming.'

The Grand Leutna paced around the table, impatient. 'You have done well, Leutna Braxx.' He thought he saw Braxx relax a little. 'Bring forward the attack plans.' Gahn held his baton before him for maximum effect. 'We are ready to strike.'

VI

PERSUASION

The Kestran President strode through the hallway of his palace, the medals of service pinned to his broad chest shining in the morning sun. Zana walked beside him as they talked. She was tall herself, but was always surprised to find herself looking up to the President on account of his towering figure.

'Yes,' the President was musing, 'a small Commando-style attack would probably have the best chance of success.' They stopped at a doorway. 'It would seem we would have little to lose.' Zana nodded in agreement. 'Has Lovell agreed to lead the mission?'

'Not yet,' the Colonel admitted.

The President stopped to look down at her. 'But he will?'

Zana ran her fingers over the flowers of a *Flora Carillon* as she thought. They responded with a soft, romantic tinkling sound. 'I believe I know his weakness, Mr President,' she said, cryptically.

Lovell was always surprised how much clearer everything felt after a shower. Stepping out of the cubicle, he wrapped himself in a towel and joined his companion in the lounge. He had to admit, the Kestran Intelligence Bureau certainly knew how to make their guests comfortable. He had even almost forgiven them for the day before.

Clarence was sitting at the breakfast table sampling some of the indigenous fruit. He grasped at a purple Tharax with a hairy hand and proceeded to pick at its soft flesh.

'Want some breakfast?' he asked as Lovell entered the room, drying his hair on a smaller towel. Lovell took the half-peeled Tharax in response, sniffed it and tossed it back

'Smells like the coffee tastes,' he grimaced. 'Don't they have eggs in this place?'

'Of course!' Clarence announced, breezily. 'Lanta eggs.'

Lovell couldn't help grimacing again. Even the word left a nasty taste in his mouth. 'Lanta?'

The chimpanzee nodded, eagerly. 'A swamp reptile.'

Lovell felt his stomach heave. 'Thanks,' he belched. 'Think I'll take a rain check.'

There was a hiss from behind him, and Lovell turned to see Colonel Zana standing in the doorway. He was not at all embarrassed to be caught in his towel.

'Good morning, Mr. Lovell,' said Zana, being careful to not let her gaze wander. She nodded towards Clarence. 'Good morning, Mr Bond.'

Lovell leaned casually against the wall and draped his hand towel around his shoulders. He hoped it was alluring. 'Morning.'

Frustratingly, Zana seemed completely immune to his advances. 'Are you being looked after?' she asked, pleasantly.

Lovell nodded. 'Thank you.'

'You slept well?'

Lovell nodded again. He knew what she was doing. 'Thank you.'

'Good.' There was a pause. 'And is the food to your liking?'

That did it. Holding tight to his towel, Lovell walked over to square up to the Colonel. Zana couldn't help notice a deep scar cutting across his chest. The legacy of one of many close encounters, she guessed.

'I am not going on that mission,' Lovell breathed, his eyes burning with a fierce determination.

'We'll see,' Zana said, simply.

The corridor was lined with heavy steel doors. Their footsteps echoed to the ceiling as Zana led the way, flanked by two Kestran guards. Lovell loped behind them, followed in turn by two more guards. At least they had allowed him to dress first. He was annoyed to find his clothes had been washed and pressed overnight.

'No trial, huh?' he protested. 'Just goodbye, Lovell?'

Zana was doing her best to ignore him.

'I thought Kestra was a civilised society!' Still, there came no reply from the Colonel. Lovell found he was having to run to keep up. 'Don't tell me,' he panted, 'if I agree to your crazy plan, then it's an immediate free pardon, right?' He might as well have been talking to himself for all the reaction he was getting. 'Well, let me tell you, Colonel, on my planet we call that blackmail.' He let the words sink in. 'Understand me? Blackmail!'

Striding ahead of him, Zana took advantage of the fact that Lovell couldn't see her and allowed herself a subdued smile.

Lovell was almost relieved when they reached the end of the corridor. His legs were beginning to tire. He was clearly out of shape. Without a word of explanation, Colonel Zana turned to the last door on the left and nodded to one of the guards. At her signal, the guard inserted a plastic code card into a slot in the wall. Lovell heard the soft whirring of gears and circuits as bolts were released in the door. Slowly, the guard swung it open and Zana turned, beckoning Lovell to enter. Summoning all the disdain he could, Lovell looked back at her for a moment before hooking his thumbs in his belt loops and walking over the threshold into the room beyond.

And then he stopped dead.

His eyes widened in amazement. This was clearly not the prison cell he had been expecting. The far wall was lined with racks of gold ingots. So taken was he with their lustre, that Lovell barely noticed the heavy door being swung shut behind him. The noise as it rammed home prompted him to snap his gaping mouth shut. He swallowed in disbelief.

'What is your weakness, Mr Lovell?'

Lovell tore his eyes away from the treasure trove before him just long enough to see that Zana and he were now alone. He gazed back at the gold. He didn't say a word. He didn't have to. The Colonel smiled, knowingly.

'There's a million in gold right in front of you, Mr Lovell. It's yours to take with you, right now.' She took a step closer. Lovell felt like prey in the clutches of a predator. 'If you help us in our mission.'

Lovell found his voice, at last. 'How do you know that I won't take the million and run?' he rasped, his mouth dry.

Colonel Zana summoned her sweetest smile. 'Because, if you did,' she began, her almond eyes twinkling, 'I would find you and kill you.'

VII

THE PLAYER IS PLAYED

Lovell's freighter sat exactly where he had last seen it. The hole in its engine had been repaired and painted, so much so that it drew the eye when compared to the rest of the ship. He almost felt embarrassed at the rusting hull plates around it. Almost.

'What changed your mind?' asked Clarence B. Bond as he settled into his seat on the flight deck.

'I was convinced on moral grounds,' replied Lovell evasively, strapping himself in for launch.

'Where do you want this?'

Lovell spun round on his seat to see two guards manhandling a heavy crate between them. It hovered an inch above the floor. Lovell could hear the gentle whine of the grav-lifts beneath it.

Suddenly in a hurry, Lovell snapped his restraints off and jumped from his seat. 'Er, right through here,' he said quickly, gesturing to the rear of the ship. As the captain led the guards through to the hold, Clarence drummed his fingers against the dash. He could swear Lovell didn't want him to know what was in that crate.

The hold was a mess. Machine parts, coils of wire and plain old junk lay strewn on the floor.

'Just leave it there, that would be great,' said Lovell quietly, keen that his co-pilot shouldn't hear. The guards maneuvered the crate to a corner where one of them bent down to switch the grav-lifts off. Suddenly heavy, the crate dropped to the floor with a thud. Lovell spun around to check that Clarence hadn't heard. 'That's great. Thanks, fellas,' he smiled as the guards retreated. He waited one minute to give the guards time to exit via the ramp to the space port, then turned to open the container. The press of a button and the lid hissed open. Lovell lifted his hand to his mouth, involuntarily. He had never seen so much gold.

'Need any help back there?'

In a sudden panic, Lovell stabbed at the controls to close the lid and wheeled round to face Clarence was hovering by the door to the hold.

'Nope,' Lovell said quickly. All good here.' He leaned against the crate as nonchalantly as he could. 'Just loading supplies.'

Clarence nodded, slowly, his wide ape eyes peering into the gloom of the hold. 'Well,' he said at last, 'we're clear for lift-off.'

'Sure,' Lovell blinked. 'Be right there.'

With a final look around, Clarence made his way back to the flight deck.

By the time Lovell joined him in the cockpit, the chimp was strapped in and ready for launch. 'Okay,' he smiled, 'take her up.'

It took Clarence moments to fire up the engines. A few deft movements, a sequence of switches thrown and they roared into life. 'Port engine's sounding good.'

'Yeah,' Lovell agreed as he gazed through a side window. 'They did a good job.'

In no time at all, they had punched through Kestra's atmosphere and into the blackness of space. The buffeting associated with atmospheric flight ceased and the freighter eased herself into a smooth flight. Or at least, as smooth as she could ever get. Despite the repairs to her engine, she still juddered alarmingly once or twice as they broke free from Kestra's orbit. Somewhere, something fell over.

Lovell took up his usual position with his feet on the dash. He cast a look at Clarence and saw that the chimp had been eyeing him with suspicion. 'Compute a course, Clarence,' he said, idly.

'Where to?' replied Clarence with caution.

Lovell couldn't help chuckling. 'Home.' He let the word sink in.

'Earth?' Clarence's eyes grew wider still.

'Sure.' Lovell leaned back dangerously in his chair, folding his arms behind his head as if ready to doze off.

'But,' Clarence spluttered, 'I thought you'd made some kind of a deal.'

Lovell reached up to pull his hat from a hook and placed it over his face. 'I told you,' he drawled, 'those Kestrans are crazy. You don't make deals with lunatics.' Reaching up again to turn out a light that was disturbing him, Lovell gave a yawn.

'I'm not so sure,' Clarence persisted. 'If you make a deal you should stick to it.'

Lovell waved a dismissive hand at his co-pilot. 'Hit the computer.' Even with his hat over his face, Lovell could tell Clarence wasn't moving. He took a deep breath and swept the hat from his face. 'What would you say to splitting a quarter of a million?'

Clarence grabbed his restraints in surprise. 'You've got a quarter of a million?'

'In gold,' Lovell smiled, conspiratorially. 'A straight split - sixty, forty.' He could see that Clarence wasn't objecting. This was going to be easier than he had thought. He swung his legs from his chair. 'I'll set the course, you make us some coffee, huh? Some *real* coffee that *tastes* like coffee.' Clapping his hirsute companion on the shoulder, Lovell made for the guidance computer. Clarence smiled his assent, snapped open his restraints and made for the living quarters.

'One coffee coming right up.'

Lovell waited for the ape to leave the flight deck before turning to the guidance computer. Reaching out, he punched at a series of buttons to set the course for Earth. He was surprised by a discordant bleep and a readout on the monitor.

'*RESET*'.

He tried again.

'*RESET*.'

Just as he was about to try a third attempt, Lovell noticed a button flashing on the comms panel. He punched it on and the frequency opened. A recorded voice squawked from the speaker.

'This is Colonel Zana,' it began, much too loud. 'To protect our investment of one million in gold bullion - ' Suddenly panicked, Lovell clamped his hands over the speaker to stop Clarence overhearing. 'We have modified your guidance computer. It will not accept navigational data taking the ship outside the limits of the galaxy.'

Lovell listened, aghast. 'Of all the - '

'The detailed plans to the fortress are in your living quarters,' Zana concluded from the panel. 'Good luck, Mr Lovell.'

Lovell snapped off the recording with a look of disgust as Clarence returned with a tray of coffee.

'Having trouble?' asked the ape in all innocence.

'Trouble?' stammered Lovell, none too convincingly. 'What trouble? Why should I have trouble?'

Clarence drew a roll of colourful acetone from an inside pocket. 'Well,' he said, holding it up before him, 'there's this.'

Lovell's mouth hung open. So many different options suddenly presented themselves. Denial. Anger. Defeat. He chose the first.

'What's that?'

Clarence stabbed at a button on the dash and a table slid out between the two pilot's chairs. Placing the tray of coffee on the table, he turned back to Lovell with narrowed eyes. 'Give it up, Lovell,' he smiled. 'You're not that good an actor.'

Lovell froze like a Gumbac caught in a searchlight. 'Huh?' he said at last.

Clarence swung himself into his seat. 'I helped set the whole thing up, Lovell. You might as well come clean.'

Lovell's head swam as he thought through the implications. 'Does that include me?' he breathed in disbelief. He found himself grabbing at an overhead bulkhead to keep his balance. 'Does that include setting *me* up?'

'Well,' Clarence replied easily, 'as a military philosopher, I must admit I was intrigued when I was approached.'

Lovell blinked. 'Approached?' he gasped. 'When?'

The chimpanzee reached for his coffee and blew on the top to cool it. Lovell could tell he was enjoying himself.

'Oh, about a month ago.'

Lovell had heard enough. Letting go the bulkhead, he swung his arm ready for a fight. 'Why, you two faced, sneaky -'

Clarence didn't even flinch. 'Me? Sneaky?' he asked in all innocence, taking a sip of his coffee. 'How about one million that suddenly became a quarter of a million?'

That stopped Lovell dead in his trucks. Of course. Clarence would know about that, too. 'Yeah, well that's, er - ' he spluttered, groping for a plausible explanation. 'I was going to tell you about that.'

'Oh, really?' Clarence looked suddenly annoyed. 'Just waiting for the right time, huh?' He shot Lovell a look of disbelief then relaxed back in his chair. 'It can be done, by the way.'

Lovell was blindsided again. This conversation was taking so many turns, he could barely keep up. 'What can be done?'

'The attack on the Zargon fortress. We can do it.'

Lovell felt subjected to a barrage of blows. Just what *didn't* Clarence know? '*We?*'

The chimp nodded. 'Why not? We make a good team. We'll need some specialist help, of course.'

Slowly, Lovell lowered himself into his seat by the flight dash. 'Specialist?'

'Sure,' replied Clarence with enthusiasm. 'Look at us. I mean,' he corrected himself, 'look at *you*.'.

Lovell allowed himself a sardonic chuckle. 'None taken,' he laughed. 'We'll need a robot.'

Clarence shrugged. 'I know where we can get one.'

'No.' Lovell was suddenly excited. 'I'll get us a robot. If we're going to do this, and I'm saying *if*, then I'm in command.'

Clarence B. Bond nodded in agreement. As ever, he was happy to let Lovell believe he was in control of events. 'Right,' he concurred.

Satisfied, Lovell flattened the roll of acetone on the table and took his coffee. 'What do you suggest?'

Clarence smiled to himself. Lovell being in command sure hadn't lasted long. 'It's difficult, but not impossible.'

Lovell leaned forward. 'Alright.' He wanted to know just how far the chimp had thought it through. 'Just for starters, where would you land?'

Suddenly in his element, Clarence stabbed at the map with a hairy finger. 'Right there.' He could tell Lovell was sceptical. 'It's the perfect place. Under their surveillance scanners but close enough to make it overland to their first line of defence.'

Lovell stared at the plans. Clarence was right. 'Er, yeah,' he bluffed. 'That's just what I would suggest. Well done.'

'You're in command, Lovell,' Clarence teased.

Lovell relaxed back in his chair. 'Why did you do it, Clarence? Why set me up to do this?'

'Because I knew you never would, otherwise. Sometimes, doing the right thing is the right thing to do. Besides,' he added with a wink, 'they got great beer.' With that, Clarence swivelled his chair to the computer console. 'So,' he said, his fingers poised over the navigation systems. 'Where to?'

Lovell kicked his feet up on the dash and leaned back in his chair. 'Let's go get us a robot.'

VIII
MEET RUDY

Clarence had never seen such a forsaken place. The barren planetoid was so out of the way as to be virtually invisible on any of the freighter's star maps. A series of low, unusually designed buildings littered the area where Lovell had set his craft down. Aside from those, there seemed to be nothing of interest.

'You sure you've brought us to the right place?' The chimp scratched his head. 'These are the experts?'

'Sure!' Lovell breezed through a door into a sterile looking reception area. A single desk sat in the middle of the floor. The woman seated behind it was filing her nails.

'Busy, huh?' Clarence remarked. He looked around the room to see they were the only visitors. If he'd had had any confidence at all in Lovell's plan, he was losing it fast.

'It's exclusive!' Lovell proclaimed as he strode towards the desk. Remarkably, the receptionist failed to even acknowledge their presence.

'Those nails must need a lot of work,' Clarence whispered beneath his breath.

Lovell smirked. 'Excuse me?' he barked, trying to attract the woman's attention. Nothing. He cleared his throat. 'Er, *excuse me?*'

Reluctantly, the receptionist stopped her filing and deigned to look up. With an expression of pure disdain, she indicated a bell on her desk then turned her attention back to her nails.

Lovell rolled his eyes. 'Seriously?' He let his hand fall on the button and the bell let out a '*ding*' that echoed around the room.

At that, the receptionist let go her nail file and sat forward in her seat. 'Can I help you, sir?' she enquired with an unexpected smile, suddenly all sweetness and light.

'Er, I made an appointment to see Mr McHine?'

The receptionist tapped at her computer keyboard.

'You know,' leered Lovell, leaning an elbow on the desk, 'you're much prettier when you smile.'

'That's funny,' replied the receptionist without a trace of humour, 'you seem much more intelligent when you're quiet.'

Clarence suppressed a snigger.

'Mr McHine will be right with you. Would you care to take a seat?' She nodded over to a plastic bench that sat by a wall. The only concession to homeliness was a picture hung on the wall, a framed print of a waterfall.

'Real nice,' Clarence remarked as he lifted himself onto the bench. A sudden thought came to him. 'Wait. *Mr McHine?*'

Lovell nodded. 'Uh huh.'

'As in *machine?*' The chimp lifted a hand to his eyes. 'That is so lame.'

'I think it's a pseudonym,' Lovell explained.

'I should certainly hope so.' Clarence looked up as an inner door opened onto the vast reception hall. A fresh-faced, sleek-haired salesman walked quickly towards them, flashing them a dazzling smile in greeting. Clarence didn't trust him one bit.

'Gentlemen, gentlemen, welcome.' McHine's voice was as loud as his suit. He threw his arms wide. 'As I always say, our aim is to please, and the customer is always - and I mean *always* - right!' If it were at all possible, Clarence thought his smile flashed even brighter. His perfect white teeth almost lit the room.

'John Lovell,' Lovell announced as he stood. 'This my colleague, Mr Bond.' Clarence nodded. If McHine was in any way thrown by being greeted by an ape, he didn't show it. Perhaps these rim worlds were more sophisticated than he had thought.

'The pleasure is all mine,' enthused McHine shaking them both vigorously by the hand. 'If you will follow me?'

As the salesman turned to walk away, Clarence was sure he saw his smile snap off. Lovell fell in behind him, giving the receptionist a cheery wink as they passed her desk. Clarence loped far enough behind to look beneath the receptionist's desk. From the waist down, she was a jumble of loose cables. Suppressing a grin, the chimp wondered just when he should tell Lovell he had made a pass at a robot.

The showroom was vast. Spread over several levels, it was home to robots of all shapes and sizes, all of them for sale. Some stood motionless. The more desperate of them waved to the small party as they entered the room, desperate to attract their attention and be picked out for a new home.

'What can I interest you in?' McHine was saying as he led them through the showroom to a mezzanine overlooking the main floor. 'A robot? Android? Does it have to be humanoid? We have the best selection in the Universe!'

He paused before a glass balustrade beyond which the mezzanine fell away to the showroom below. Lovell peered over to see another salesman showing a robot to an alien family. Catching sight of the salesman's eyes, Lovell could see he looked just like McHine's twin brother.

'Do let me know if you see anything here that catches your eye!' He spread his arms wide, then gestured to an alcove nearby. 'This, for example, is a very good all-purpose model.' He led Lovell and Clarence over to a robot on a small display stand. McHine snapped his fingers and the robot began to effortlessly juggle three balls at tremendous speed.

'Excellent coordination,' admitted Clarence, grudgingly.

'Ah,' grinned McHine, 'the secret's in the highly refined visual circuits.'

'Not sure we'd have much call for juggling though.' Clarence smiled back, obligingly.

Lovell decided to take control of the conversation. 'Forgive my companion, Mr McHine.' He gave a sideways look of warning to Clarence. 'It's just that we're looking for something a little more robust.' Throwing an arm around the salesman, Lovell led him back to the balcony. 'You know, I once saw an R42 working on a construction site - '

The words had an immediate effect on McHine. No sooner were they out of Lovell's mouth than the salesman came to a sudden halt. McHine struggled to keep his composure as he replied.

'The R42?' he sputtered. 'I'm afraid we don't stock that particular model. I'm sure sir could do much better than the R42.'

Clarence leaned in, mischievously. 'The customer is always right. Right?' he winked.

McHine stood still for a moment, clearly unsure how to proceed. At last, he relented. 'Do you know, I think we may have an R42 after all? It must have slipped my mind.'

'Yes,' agreed Lovell, slapping the salesman playfully on the back. 'It must.'

If it were possible, McHine's smile was even less sincere than before. 'If you will follow me, gentlemen.'

In contrast to the quiet reception room and sales floor, the factory area was a hive of activity. Clarence guessed there were such high margins on the robots that they only had to sell a few to meet their overheads. Given that, perhaps a rim world was the perfect location for such a business. The ape looked around at the long assembly lines as he walked behind the two men. At intervals, robots were being assembled and repaired by other robots. Spare parts whizzed past on conveyor belts. Every now and then, a shower of sparks arced into the air. Leading his customers through to an assembly area, McHine looked back to see Lovell's interest had been caught by a robot on the assembly line. It was of a strange, angular construction with a large head bristling with aerials and antennae. A smaller service droid was busy programming the robot's speech circuits. The robot looked at Lovell almost quizzically.

'Pop ita pap ata pop it?' it asked as the smaller droid attended its speech centres. 'Put uta pat putta pit?'

Seeing Lovell's blank expression, McHine felt it his duty to oblige him with an explanation. 'It's a specialist order for the Popatia Ambassador,' he announced. 'Interesting language, only two consonants.'

Lovell nodded, already thinking of the rudest riposte he could make with just two consonants. Luckily, and rather improbably, he was interrupted by a sudden burst of music. Spinning round, he saw a slender robot wearing a tailcoat and white gloves. It had a supercilious expression painted on its face and its head was topped off with a precarious looking wig of jet-black hair. It was seated at a futuristic electronic piano, his front panel removed to expose a mess of intricate circuitry. Another service droid picked up a probe to make an adjustment, then the robot leaned over the keyboard again. As its mechanical fingers danced across the keyboard, it progressed through a piece of music that Lovell was sure he recognised. As it reached a climax, however, the robot hit a bum note. And then another. Alerted by the discord, the service droid leaned forward with his probe. The robot stopped playing and sat back to be corrected. Lovell looked around. 'I don't see any R42,' he said.

McHine hesitated before a bay door. 'You're sure I can't tempt you to consider some other model?' he asked, hopefully.

Lovell's eyes narrowed. He'd had enough of this guy's evasiveness. 'Why would you want to do that?'

'No reason,' the salesman said, quickly. Almost too quickly, thought Lovell. 'No reason at all.' He gestured through the door as it slid open with a hum. 'Through here gentlemen.'

McHine led the way through the doorway into what appeared to be a storeroom. In contrast to the immaculately gleaming showroom and the clinical manufacturing and assembly area, it was dimly lit and cluttered with obsolete and broken bits of circuitry of all shapes and sizes. Clarence was sure he saw robotic shapes standing eerily in the gloom.

'Here we are, gentlemen,' McHine called, nervously. He stood aside and gestured feebly to a corner. There, stood a metallic giant. Over seven feet high, with giant tree trunk legs and a massive body, the R42 had several minor dents in the arms. Its metal casing was dirty and, in places, caked in rust. The giant robot stood on a low circular dais raised a few inches from the floor, a faint column of light rising up from the floor around it. Clarence was not impressed.

'Is that it?' He reached between the buttons of his tunic to scratch at his chest.

McHine looked hurt. 'It has much to commend it, sir. Positronic power, completely self generating.'

'Then, why were you so keen to put us off seeing it?' Lovell sneered.

Clarence was walking around the platform. 'Could do with a new paint job.'

McHine sniffed, indignant. 'That'll polish up, sir. If you decide to buy we'll have it cleaned up and thoroughly checked out.'

'Sounds fair enough.' Lovell moved forward to touch the great metal beast before him.

'Please don't touch it, sir.' McHine twitched alarmingly, his grin more rictus than ever. 'It's immobilised at present.'

Lovell stopped dead in his tracks and turned to face the salesman. 'Problems?' He noticed McHine couldn't even meet his gaze.

'Not exactly, sir,' the salesman fawned. 'It's just that this model is highly specialised. We only ever made three.'

'Not a popular model, then?' asked Clarence, pointedly. He was beginning to regret giving Lovell his head. If it had been up to him, they would have found a perfectly serviceable robot in one of the busier space malls of Delphin Three.

'There are sometimes a few minor flaws,' McHine admitted reluctantly.

Lovell's eyebrows rose. 'Flaws?' He could tell McHine was being deliberately obstructive.

'Well,' the salesman coughed, 'let's say it isn't really suitable for intricate, delicate work.'

Lovell laughed and cast a look to Clarence. 'We didn't plan to use it to count eggs.' The chimp joined him in a knowing smile. Turning back to the robot, Lovell noticed that McHine had taken a step closer.

'May I ask what you do plan to use it for?' His voice was low and accusatory.

Lovell thought for a moment. 'I'd say more in the line of a demolition function.'

McHine looked relieved to hear it. 'Oh, well why didn't you say?' he boomed, his arms wide. Suddenly he was all smiles.

'You didn't ask,' replied Clarence, simply.

'Demolition?' The salesman had turned back to look into the R42 before him. 'You couldn't do better.'

Lovell scratched at his chin. He looked to his companion for guidance. Clarence shrugged. So much for Lovell being in command. *It's up to you*, he said with a look.

'Okay,' Lovell said at last. 'We'll take it.'

McHine was clearly elated to have made the sale. 'Ah! Very good, sir. I'm sure you won't be disappointed.' He rubbed his hands together in the universal symbol for one expecting a large amount of money.

'We'd like to rent. And we'd like to take it with us.'

McHine's face fell. 'That could be a problem,' he said, suddenly worried. 'We'd prefer to have our engineers check it out first. You could pick it up in a day or so.'

Lovell was adamant. 'We need to take it *now*,' he said with some force.

McHine sighed. 'In that case it would have to be without our guarantee or insurance cover.'

What an odd thing to say, thought Clarence. He caught Lovell looking at him for support. *Whatever*, he said with a shrug. Lovell broke into a broad grin and clapped McHine on the shoulder again.

'We'll take it!'

McHine seemed caught between satisfaction at the sale and concern at the implications. 'Any damage or accidents - ' he persisted.

'Yeah, right,' Lovell clearly wasn't listening. Reaching into his pocket he pulled out a battered wallet and withdrew his credit card. 'I'm sure this'll make you feel a little better.'

Faced with hard plastic, McHine's concerns seemed to disappear. He flashed his slickest smile. 'On a used item like this, I could make you a very good purchase deal.'

'I'm sure you could,' Lovell replied, 'and the interest would kill me.' He held out his card. 'We rent. Or it's no deal.'

McHine considered his options then gave an awkward bow. 'Of course,' he said, obsequiously. 'Excuse me one moment.' With that, he walked through the bay door and back towards the reception area to process the sale.

Lovell turned to Clarence with a sigh. 'What do you think?'

Clarence rested on his knuckles. 'I can't say I'm impressed.'

But Clarence could tell Lovell wasn't listening. He was walking round the robot, oblivious to his caution. 'This thing can walk through a steel door. See that casing? It's damn near indestructible.' He whistled, admiringly. Running his fingers idly over a small control unit beside the platform, he looked up at the column of light that rose from the floor. 'Electro forcefield,' he muttered to himself. Before Clarence could stop him, he had reached towards the control panel and pressed a large, red button. *Typical*, thought Clarence. *He just can't help himself.* Suddenly, as if released from captivity, the R42 let out an almighty roar. Lovell stumbled back as the hulk before him stretched itself up to its full height.

Clarence watched as a light appeared in the robot's eyes. Worryingly, he could hear the sound of servos and gears engaging as if it were preparing to move.

Lovell had fallen to the floor in surprise. 'Er, Clarence?' he simpered. 'I don't think I should have pressed that button.'

Clarence was backing away into an alcove as the robot powered up. 'D'you think?' he replied with a sneer. Raising his hairy hands, he peeked through his fingers in fear.

With a discordant mechanical roar, the robot jumped forward and off its display platform, crashing into a pile of mechanical parts on the floor. With a hum of motors, its huge head turned to stare menacingly at Clarence and Lovell.

'Don't suppose that thing has an off switch?' pleaded Clarence, his back to the wall.

Lovell sprung back to the control panel in search of a power switch. 'What if I make it worse?' he shouted above the din.

The robot swung a heavy mechanical arm at a shelf of cables, sending it sprawling the length of the workshop.

'How could it possibly be any worse?' Clarence bellowed in fear.

As the robot looked around for its next target, a loud speaker in the ceiling above crackled into life.

'Mr Lovell?' came McHine's voice. Clarence could tell he was smiling. 'Your credit has been cleared. You've rented yourself a robot!' The speaker snapped off as the robot lumbered forward. The ground seemed to shake with every step. As Lovell skirted the wall to join Clarence in his alcove, the R42 lifted its arm again. With a mighty effort, it sent a pile of scrap crashing into a deactivated droid across the room.

Noticing the robot focusing its attention on Lovell, Clarence began to back slowly away from his companion. 'I think it's you he wants.'

Lovell turned to reply, only to see that Clarence was now some distance away. He had left Lovell completely exposed. 'Thanks,' he hissed, bitterly. '*Partner.*'

Holding up his hands, Lovell attempted to calm the mechanical beast. 'Take it easy,' he soothed. 'Easy...' In response, the robot took another juddering step forward, bearing down on Lovell from his great height. 'Do something!' Lovell screamed in panic.

Clarence looked about him for inspiration. 'I'll go get help!' he shouted at last, scurrying through the dock door on his knuckles.

Menacingly, the robot raised an arm. Lovell had already seen the damage the R42 could do with that arm. He trembled in fear in the alcove, convinced every breath he took would be his last. Just as the robot prepared to smash its arm down, Lovell saw his chance. Curling himself up into a ball, he rolled straight between the robot's legs as it brought its weight to bear on a set of shelves near where Lovell had been cowering. Scrambling to his feet, Lovell skidded across the floor and flung himself though the bay door, punching at its controls as he slid through. The shutter slammed shut behind him and Lovell breathed a sigh of relief. Looking around for Clarence, he wiped the beads of sweat from his face with the back of his hand. A sudden wrenching sound from behind made him jump out of his skin. Lovell whirled round just in time to see the huge robot wrenching the door from its mountings. Tossing the sheet metal aside as if it were nothing more than a piece of paper, it stepped through the gaping hole in the wall with a mechanical roar.

'You know it's rude to come in without knocking?' Lovell sneered. Seeing the robot squaring up to him again, the captain did what he always did in a tight spot. He turned and ran.

Hurdling piles of mechanical detritus, Lovell hurtled down the corridor. If he was uncertain where it was leading, he was certain soon enough. It was leading nowhere. Lovell found himself coming to a shuddering halt before a dead end. 'Who builds a corridor that goes nowhere?' he shouted to no one in particular. From behind, came the lumbering footsteps of the R42. It was closing fast. Turning to face it, Lovell saw that he had run past a series of steel doors in the sides of the corridor. A worrying thought occurred to him. If he wanted to try those doors, he'd have to run *towards* the robot. Looking around him, he saw there was no other way. Lovell took a deep breath. Bunching his fists, he launched himself back down the corridor, right into the path of the oncoming metal brute. As the robot bellowed in surprise, Lovell screamed in response. At last he found himself at the nearest door. Punching at the control button, he was met with a discordant bleep. Locked. Lovell swore under his breath. The robot was just feet away now, but he had to try another door. Sprinting across to the adjacent wall, he stabbed frantically at the controls. Locked. Cursing his luck, he cast a glance up the corridor. There was time to try just one more door before the robot was upon him. Always one to run from danger, it took another mighty effort of will for Lovell to run *towards* the hulking beast. The robot's arm was flailing about it as it moved remorselessly down the corridor. Suddenly, Lovell saw what he must do. As the mighty arm swung towards him, he grabbed at the heavy hand attachment and hung on for dear life. Confused, the robot swung its arm dangerously about it, fighting hard to keep its balance. Lovell could smell the distinctive tang of grease and servo oil. Swinging high into the air, Lovell chose his moment to let go. Just as the robot flung its arm behind, Lovell released his hold and arced through the air towards the door. He landed with a little less grace than he might have wanted, but he had bought himself time. As the robot turned to continue its relentless pursuit, Lovell planted his fist into the control panel by the door. With a happy bleep, and much to Lovell's relief, it swung open. 'Third time's a charm!' Lovell laughed as he flung himself inside, punching at the interior controls. Just as the robot reached him, the door swung shut with a slam.

Lovell leaned back against the wall, breathing hard. He pinched the bridge of his nose. 'It's okay, buddy,' he told himself. 'You made it.' It took it a moment to realise he was standing in complete darkness. Groping for a light switch, he fought hard to keep himself calm. At last he flicked a switch and light flooded the room. He blinked into the glare. There, in front of him, stood a mop in a bucket. A shelf of cleaning products ran the length of the wall. In a corner, a pair of discarded rubber gloves lay on the floor. He was in the cleaning cupboard. There was nowhere to go. For a minute or more, Lovell could hear the robot thrashing about in the corridor beyond. Then, there was silence. Hesitantly, Lovell pressed his ear to the door. Nothing. Just as he was certain the robot had gone, the wall gave way beside him. Clearly choosing to disregard the door, the R42 had smashed his way into the cupboard through the brickwork. Debris filled the space within moments so that Lovell was soon choking in the dust. He could feel he was growing weaker every second. He doubted he had the strength to run any more. As the dust settled, the robot looked around. It saw Lovell cowering against the rear wall and tensed its metal sinews. Lovell's legs buckled beneath him. He squeezed his eyes tight shut as the lumbering giant stomped ever closer, its arm outstretched.

Never thought it would end in a maintenance cupboard, he thought as he prepared himself for the end. But nothing happened. Opening first one eye and then the other, Lovell was astonished to see the robot had simply stopped.

'Thank you, sir,' came a rasping, mechanical voice. 'Thank you for hiring me.' The R42 extended its hand towards Lovell's. Astonishingly, Lovell felt himself returning the gesture.

'Er, sure,' he replied, confused. 'You're welcome.'

'Your receipt for the damage.'

McHine tore a strip of paper from the readout on his desk. The reception area was as quiet as ever. Even as he was handed his receipt, Lovell couldn't help but make eyes with the receptionist beside the salesman.

Clarence ambled up beside him. 'Everything okay?'

'No thanks to you,' Lovell grunted. He held up the receipt so the chimp could see the rows of numbers. Very large numbers. Clarence whistled. 'If you can call that okay.'

The chimpanzee puffed out his cheeks and scratched his head. 'Well, there was that door, and the hole in the wall.'

McHine had walked from his desk towards the now inert form of the R42. 'He should be fine now,' he grinned with all the fake sincerity he could muster. 'Just got a little over-excited.'

Lovell frowned. 'A robot can get over-excited?'

'This one certainly can,' interjected Clarence, casting a wary eye over the robot's bulk.

'The R42 is an extremely advanced model,' explained McHine, patiently.

Lovell nodded. 'Switch him on,' he said, at last.

'Gladly.' As Clarence hid behind Lovell's legs, McHine leaned over and reached between the robot's chest plates. There was a gentle hum and the R42 stretched itself up in readiness. Its eyes blazed as it looked around.

'You got a name?' Lovell asked.

The robot cocked its head. 'My last owner from Earth called me Nureyev.' Its voice was rough and guttural.

'Nureyev?'

The robot nodded. 'After the Russian ballet dancer, Rudolph Nureyev. He was known for his grace and elegance.'

Lovell shot a look to Clarence. He could tell the chimp was enjoying the joke.

'Okay,' Lovell grinned. 'Rudy it is.'

IX

PAX SEMPER

Lovell's freighter rattled as it skimmed through the tail of a comet. 'Slip-drifting' he called it, in the mistaken belief that it provided his sluggish craft with a kick of speed. That may be so, thought Clarence as he wrestled with the controls, but it also led to the intakes being filled with dust. Which meant they'd need a maintenance stop sooner or later. It was a false economy but then, he guessed, Lovell had been guilty of far worse. Gripping the control column, Clarence bounced the old freighter off the comet's tail and away from the rim world. As he settled back in his chair, he turned to see Lovell was fast asleep in his. He was awoken by a crash from the flight deck door. Springing forward in surprise, he lifted his hands to rub some feeling back into his face, then caught Clarence's eye.

'What?' Lovell said, innocently. 'I was just resting my eyes.'

Rudy's huge hand hove into view. 'Your coffee, sir,' he rasped.

Lovell looked up at the great mechanical beast just as his metal foot caught on a stray piece of cabling on the floor. Rudy swung his free arm to try and maintain his balance, but succeeded only in smashing it through a control panel on the ship's starboard side. A shower of sparks lit the cockpit and a cloud of smoke rose into the air. Reaching out to break his fall, Rudy lunged for the dash, breaking the cup as his hand grasped at a monitor for support. Coffee dripped from the floor as Rudy straightened himself.

'I'm soaked,' bleated Lovell, his shirt and trousers stained brown.

'Accidents will happen,' smirked Clarence from the co-pilot's chair. Lovell noticed his pristine white tunic hadn't been touched.

'I'm sorry, sir,' said Rudy, his eyes downcast to the floor.

'You crushed the damned cup!' Lovell pointed to distorted plastic lying on the floor.

'I'll clean up the mess right away, sir.' Rudy almost bowed as he backed away towards the door.

'No, leave it,' said Lovell, springing to his feet. He suddenly felt sorry for the robot. Despite his size, he was obviously of a sensitive disposition. 'Look, er, why don't you go back, sit down and relax.'

'Yes, sir, thank you, sir.'

'And you don't need to keep thanking me.'

'No, sir.' Rudy bowed again. 'Thank you, sir.'

Lovell rolled his eyes as Rudy lumbered back into the living quarters, then threw himself back into his seat next to Clarence.

'You want me to set a course?' asked the chimp.

Lovell was using an oily rag to wipe the coffee from the dash. 'Yeah, Pax Semper.'

Clarence raised his eyebrows as he reached for the navigation panel. 'The Free Planet? It's full of eccentrics.'

Lovell glared at him, suddenly impatient. 'Well then, I guess you'll fit right in. Besides,' he added, wringing the coffee from his shirt, 'there's one eccentric we need.'

The tunnel had been drilled right through the rock beneath the mountain. As his eyes adjusted to the gloom, Clarence could even see the marks in the rock left by the huge excavators. The walls glistened with minerals and, occasionally, ran with water. More than once, Clarence had to suck the moisture from his knuckles as he walked. Ahead of him sauntered Lovell, humming tunelessly. Clarence could only hope he knew where they were headed.

At last, they emerged into an underground cavern. Judging from the size, Clarence guessed they were in the very heart of the mountain. He whistled at the sight before him. A beautiful natural cavern stretched as far as the eye could see, columns of rock giving it the air of a subterranean cathedral. Over by a particularly impressive formation of crystal and rock sat a man, completely motionless, his back to them. He was so still as to seem almost made of rock himself. Sitting cross-legged in a pose of deep meditation, he sported a shaved head and a simple, sleeveless robe that fell from his shoulders. Sitting in perfect stillness, there was a sense of potential about him like a coiled spring. His whole aura was one of both strength and tranquillity.

As Lovell and Clarence approached the man from the rear, a voice pierced the stillness. 'John Lovell!' the man exclaimed, though he'd yet to turn round. Clarence looked about him. There was no way the man could have seen them approaching. Lovell walked round to face the man on the floor. Clarence thought he recognised Oriental features as the strange figure looked up at them both.

'Sumara!' said Lovell at last, a broad grin spreading across his face. 'It's been a long time!' He gestured to the chimpanzee beside him. 'This is Clarence B. Bond.'

The man nodded, slowly, an enigmatic expression passing over his face. 'I know,' he said.

Clarence couldn't help noticing Sumara's slender fingers as they worked expertly to prepare a hot drink for his guests. Using some dried moss that he plucked from the cave walls, he set a tiny fire to make a kind of herbal tea. His movements were deft, graceful and beautifully co-ordinated. He barely seemed to touch the ground as he walked towards Lovell with a small cup. Clarence took his with a smile, appreciative of the ornately carved vessel he had been offered. Cupping the infusion in both hands, the three of them drank as one, their actions having a strange sense of ritual about them.

'It's good,' the chimp remarked as he drank. 'And sweet.'

Sumara remained impassive.

Suddenly clearing his throat, Lovell placed his cup on the floor where he lay sprawled on a heap of furs. 'We have a mission,' he announced. 'We would like you to join us.'

Sumara remained his inscrutable self.

'I must tell you,' Lovell continued, 'that we could all be killed.'

Sumara gave the slightest nod. 'Death is of no consequence,' he said, profoundly. 'And so the *threat* of death is of no consequence.'

Lovell nodded politely as if in understanding. Clarence could see the philosophical nature of the debate was already going clear over his head. Lovell ploughed on. 'The mission is to attack a fortress. A Zargon fortress.'

'Pax Semper is a Free Planet.' Sumara lowered his cup to his lap. 'We do not recognise nationality.'

'The Zargons threaten the planet of Kestra,' Clarence chipped in. 'They intend to destroy it unless we can destroy the fortress first.'

Lovell leaned forward. 'Will you join us?'

Sumara closed his eyes in thought, enabling Lovell to sneak Clarence a quick look. *What more can I do?* he said with a shrug of his shoulders.

'My head says no,' said Sumara, his eyes snapping open. 'But my heart says maybe.'

Lovell was getting impatient. 'We need an answer, Sumara.'

Sumara sighed in response. 'Then, my answer is that *no* is stronger than *maybe*.'

Lovell frowned. 'Huh? Sorry, is that a yes or - '

'It's a no, Lovell,' Clarence snapped. 'It's clearly a no.'

'I am sorry, John Lovell.' Sumara downed the last of his tea in the ensuing silence. Lovell nodded in resignation and gestured to Clarence that they should leave.

'Thanks for tea,' Lovell said ruefully as he handed Sumara his cup.

The strange man inclined his head in acknowledgement. 'I will accompany you to your ship and see your departure.'

The freighter had been parked in a bay at Pax Semper's busiest space port. A large, circular structure, it was home to an open central area with a series of launch pads arranged around its rim. The passenger lounges, customs and security offices were all housed in elegant, glass buildings.

As Lovell, Clarence and Sumara sat in a lounge awaiting a departure slot, they watched as a small private space hopper lifted off into the night sky. Feeling glum, Lovell leaned forward to rest his head in his hands. He had spent most of their walk to the space port pleading with Sumara to join them in their cause. At every turn in the rock and the conversation, the mystic had politely but firmly declined. Finally, Lovell had given up, and the rest of the journey had taken place in an uneasy silence.

Lovell looked idly around the lounge and saw a group of Zargon soldiers entering. Pulling the brim of his hat over his eyes, he sunk down in his seat to watch. Four of the soldiers found seats while two others headed to the bar area, lifting their visors to make their order.

'Clarence,' Lovell said, suddenly, 'I think we should go check our launch time.'

As Clarence opened his mouth to protest, Lovell grabbed him firmly by the arm and dragged him away. 'But we checked it when we landed,' the chimp protested. 'And that *hurts*.'

Now some distance from Sumara, Lovell nodded towards the soldiers for the first time.

'What are they doing here?' Clarence whispered.

'Like the man said,' Lovell sneered, 'it's a free planet.'

The man and chimp watched as the soldiers were served their drinks.

'Follow my lead,' Lovell whispered, suddenly.

'Wait, what?' Clarence began, but Lovell was on the move. Before the chimp could react further, his companion had bumped into a soldier at his table, spilling his drink into his lap. The soldier slowly turned to face him.

'I think you should buy me another drink,' he looked Lovell up and down with disdain. 'Earthman.'

Lovell thrust his lantern jaw into the man's face. 'Drop dead.'

The soldier's eyes blazed.

Catching Lovell's eye, Clarence waded in. 'It was your fault, you clumsy freak.'

There was an ominous silence as the four soldiers looked at each other, then they broke out into cruel laughter. 'And *he* called *me* a freak!' guffawed the soldier with the drink in his lap. Suddenly the laughter ceased and the soldier snapped to his feet. Grabbing Clarence by the scruff of his neck, he pulled him up from the floor until they were face to face. 'Who are you calling freak, *freak*?' he hissed.

Clarence's short legs kicked the air in vain. 'Let go of me, you big ape!'

Across the departure lounge, Sumara heard Clarence's raised voice. His eyes flicked over to the tables where the confrontation was unfolding, his face impassive.

The soldier threw Clarence aside as Lovell jumped forward. Putting his weight behind his fist, the captain rammed it up and into the soldier's jaw. Reeling from the blow, the Zargon raised his hand to quieten his squad. 'I'm okay,' he breathed, spitting blood to the floor. 'But I think we ought to teach these two a lesson they won't forget.'

As if they had been waiting for their chance, two of the soldier's colleagues lurched from their seats, eager to join the fight. Hoisting himself from the floor where he had been thrown, Clarence picked up a chair and swung it hard into one of the soldier's shins. The man groaned with pain but lunged forward as he fell to catch Lovell by the knees. His legs buckling beneath him, Lovell fell to the floor, his head cracking against the smooth, ceramic tiles. Dazed but not defeated, Lovell rose quickly to his feet and, with a roar, threw himself back into the fray.

Watching the fight with a detached interest from across the room, Sumara sat, his face unreadable.

The soldier that Lovell had first accosted had him pinned to the floor with a massive boot to the chest. Another held Clarence to the wall by his throat. The chimp grabbed at the man's fist, trying desperately to prise his fingers open. Seeing him squirm helplessly before him, the soldier smiled savagely as he applied even more pressure to Clarence's neck. Not convinced the plan was working, Clarence cast a fevered glance to Sumara's table, but the strange man had simply disappeared.

Now fighting two soldiers at once, Lovell was taking a beating. As one held him by the arms from behind, the other landed repeated blows on his skull. Suddenly, a voice cut through the commotion.

'ENOUGH!'

Sumara stood as impassive as ever, but his eyes blazed with a dangerous potential. The soldiers looked around, confused.

'Where the hell did he come from?' blustered the man with his hand at Clarence's throat. The chimpanzee felt his grip loosen a little as he spoke.

Their leader strode forward, panting. 'Stay out of this,' he warned. 'Wouldn't want to get your robe dirty now, would ya?'

'I said *enough*.' Stepping forward with a slow, almost lazy movement, Sumara pushed the soldier away. The Zargon staggered back, surprised at the force behind the harmless looking push. His colleagues were with him now, suddenly aware of this new threat. Clarence, having been dropped to the floor, circled round to stand with Lovell at Sumara's side. The two groups squared up to each other, three against four. Good odds, thought Clarence, though the soldiers were armed. And itching for a fight.

Sumara held his hands before him, palms pressed together, and bowed. 'Allow me, John Lovell,' he said, his voice steady.

'Right.'

To Clarence's surprise, Lovell took him by the arm and led him away to a nearby table. 'What are you trying to do?' he spluttered, rubbing at his neck with a hairy hand.

Lovell smiled, knowingly. 'I always did like an unfair fight.' With that, Lovell took a seat and leaned casually back to enjoy the action.

Over towards the centre of the lounge, the soldiers were spreading themselves into a circle surrounding Sumara. The mystic was standing stock still, his hands still pressed together as if in prayer. 'I must ask you all to leave,' he said, quietly but firmly. The soldiers laughed in response but it was hollow, as if somehow they recognised the dangerous, smouldering menace in Sumara's outward calm. Then one of them lunged forward, swinging his bunched fists viciously. Lovell and Clarence watched on from their ringside seats as Sumara swayed almost imperceptibly to one side and the blow went harmlessly past. Taking his cue, another Zargon leapt behind Sumara's back. Beyond his field of vision, the soldier aimed a hammer chop on the back of Sumara's neck. The mystic half turned, catching the soldier's arm mid-blow and using the man's own momentum to send him sprawling into the tables. Now the soldiers rushed at Sumara together. Like a spring uncoiling, Sumara unleashed himself on his attackers. The nearest received three lightning blows in quick succession from the flat of his hand. From his seat, Clarence could barely keep up with the action. It seemed Sumara was moving so fast he was a blur. First, he dealt a sickening blow to a chin with the heel of his foot, then he was punching, kicking and throwing bodies to the floor, all at lightning speed and all without apparent effort. Sumara's face looked as calm as it had when he was meditating in the cave.

'Fantastic,' whistled Clarence in admiration.

'Yeah,' agreed Lovell.

The one soldier still standing had clearly had enough. Lovell recognised him as the man whose drink he had spilled. Nursing a bruise under his eye, he stumbled away to where his pack had been left on the table. Snapping open the lid, he pulled out his HE Gun and took aim. Clarence jumped up in alarm, ready to warn Sumara to take cover.

'Hey' soothed Lovell, placing a restraining hand on his shoulder.

'But he's going for his gun.'

'Relax.' Lovell was grinning from ear to ear 'Just enjoy the show.'

The three soldiers on the floor had recovered enough by now to stagger to their feet. Seeing what was happening, they backed away to allow their comrade a clear line of fire. Sumara turned to face the soldier with the gun. The trooper lifted the weapon to his shoulder to take aim, a sickly grin spreading over his face. Calmly, Sumara subtly altered his position. He crouched into a low stance, turning sideways to his adversary. Bizarrely, his eyes were closed. Tiny beads of sweat glistened on his skin. He grit his teeth with the effort. The soldier squeezed at the trigger and his HE Gun began to whine in preparation for the shot. Suddenly, from all of twenty feet away, Sumara chopped at the air with a hand. The soldier let his gun clatter to the floor, clutching suddenly at his shoulder in pain. Clarence looked quizzically at his companion.

'Advanced telekinesis,' Lovell explained with a knowing wink.

The soldier was staring at Sumara in disbelief. Looking around him, he saw his comrades were hesitating, not quite sure how to respond. Finally, the soldier ducked to retrieve his gun from the floor. Sumara became a whirl. At breath-taking speed, he threw a series of punches and chops into the air. The soldier staggered under the force of each blow from halfway across the room, a look of sheer bemusement on his bruised face. Finally, as Sumara delivered one final blow, he fell to the floor, unconscious.

Lovell stood to applaud in wild appreciation. 'That's what you call throwing a punch!' he called, before whistling through his fingers.

The remaining soldiers stood in a line, clearly terrified, staring at Sumara as he turned to face them. Clarence noticed their eyes flick to their gun packs on the table, but they were too far away to be of any use. Still in his telekinetic stance, Sumara gestured as if he were lifting something from the floor. Slowly, inexplicably, the unconscious soldier's gun rose into the air. Hovering several feet before them, the gun swivelled to take aim at the soldiers. Slowly, they began their retreat. As one, they carefully backed away from the gun, lifted their packs from the table and left their unconscious companion behind them. Soon they running through the door to the space port beyond, no doubt keen to be on the first hopper off Pax Semter.

His task complete, Sumara relaxed his stance and the gun fell to the floor. Lovell and Clarence were beside him at once. The chimp's eyes were wider than ever and he was practically jumping with excitement.

'That was great!' he beamed. 'I've never seen anything like it.'

Sumara turned to Lovell, the faintest frown on his otherwise smooth face. 'Those men,' he began. 'I could sense their spirits.' He screwed up his eyes. 'Nothing but darkness.'

'Such men must be stopped,' interjected Clarence, carefully.

Sumara nodded, as if a decision had been made. 'Such men must be fought.'

Lovell clapped his hand on his friend's shoulder. 'Zargons,' he said. 'And there's plenty more where we're going.'

X

CARAVAN

'**M**y main problem seems to be that I can't pick up anything fragile.'

Sumara had found himself sitting with Rudy in the transport's living quarters. The great metal hulk had perched himself precariously on a low sofa by a table. He looked as despondent as any robot could. Looking around for an object to demonstrate his predicament, he reached for a small metal container. It was far from what would normally be considered as fragile. Sumara watched as Rudy tried hard to apply as little pressure as possible, but it was to no avail. The container crumpled in Rudy's hand as if it were paper. 'See what I mean?' the robot said, sadly.

Sumara took the buckled metal from the table. 'It is a simple matter of coordination,' he soothed. 'You have a mind?'

Rudy shifted his weight on the sofa, stung by the question. 'Of course,' he huffed. 'I have a very advanced brain, actually. For a demolition unit.'

Sumara nodded sympathetically. 'Then it is simply a question of imposing your will on the power of your actions.'

Rudy's eyes shone bright. 'I've never really thought of it like that before.'

'Ah,' the mystic twinkled. 'But then, you've probably never met anyone quite like me before.'

Up on the flight deck, Clarence and Lovell had swivelled their chairs to face the door to the living quarters.

'They make quite a pair,' Clarence smiled as he unbuckled himself from the harness. Now in deep space, the freighter was running smooth. Or at least, as smooth as it ever could.

'Yeah,' beamed Lovell as he turned back to the dash. He reached out to smooth the acetone plans of the Zargon fortress. 'Well,' he sighed, we've almost got a team.'

'Yeah,' agreed Clarence cynically. 'I'd say the odds are down to a thousand to one against.'

'We just need one more. Someone who can give us the edge over the Zargons.' Lovell scratched his chin. 'Someone who can see trouble ahead.'

'Oh?' asked Clarence, his eyebrows raised. 'And where will we find such a person?'

Lovell reached over the dashboard and pointed through the windshield to the black void beyond. Clarence could suddenly make out a string of small craft hanging, stationary, in the darkness. 'There!'

The Drifters' space caravan comprised a motley collection of highly decorated space vehicles. Some had obviously been assembled from parts of different origin, but all were brightly coloured. No one ship looked like another. Grouped together to form a makeshift colony joined with ramshackle moorings and tubes, they made for an impressive sight.

'Prepare to dock,' barked Lovell as the freighter approached the caravan.

'With the Drifters?' The tremor in the chimp's voice betrayed more than a little concern.

Lovell shot him a look. 'We're all drifters.'

There was a gentle jolt as the freighter connected with one of the larger craft, and Lovell headed to the rear of the ship to find his EVA suit.

Soon, he was crossing the small distance between his vehicle and the Drifter's craft, small blasts from his propulsion unit propelling him with remarkable precision towards an entrance hatch. Once through the airlock, he removed his helmet and backpack, leaving them by the door for his return. The walls in the corridor before him were covered in brightly coloured murals of ultra modern art.

'I don't know much about art,' he scoffed, 'but I know what I like.' His eye fell upon a particularly gaudy example. 'And what I don't.'

Walking carefully through the corridor, he found himself at an arched opening. Pushing aside a heavy, beaded curtain, he stumbled into a large room lit by scented candles. A mist swirled about the floor. From somewhere, Lovell could hear the tinkling of tiny bells accompanied by mysterious, calming music.

'Do not be afraid,' came an inhuman voice from the gloom. 'Come forward.'

As Lovell stepped further into the room, he found himself confronted by the sight of a very old woman sitting at a circular, glass-topped table. A light shone up through the glass, accentuating the lines and shadows on her ancient face.

'Come closer,' the woman beckoned, her voice a tuneless, mechanical rasp. 'I can feel your destiny hanging in the air.'

Lovell frowned as he approached her, only to see the woman holding a small device to her throat. 'It's John Lovell,' he beamed.' You can cut the sales crap, Dorita, you old fake.'

With that, the music stopped. Bright lights snapped on in the ceiling. Dorita dropped the device from her neck as she recognised the man before her. 'Lovell, you old skin!' Her voice, though cracked with age, was suddenly soft and feminine. 'You might have told me!'

Rising from her chair, the old woman lunged forward to embrace her old friend. As Lovell chuckled, Dorita walked the circumference of the room, snuffing out the candles as she went. 'Help me will you?' she said, looking back at Lovell. 'Never could stand the smell of these damned things.'

'You're looking stiff,' the captain remarked as he moved to her assistance.

Dorita flashed him a look. 'So will you when you reach a hundred and thirty eight.'

Lovell stopped dead in his tracks. 'You're not - ?' he gasped.

'Sure am.' Dorita puffed out her chest in pride, then immediately clutched at her back with a wince of pain.

'That young, eh?' chuckled Lovell, impressed.

Dorita smiled, revealing as many gaps as teeth. 'Drink?'

Lovell nodded gratefully as she moved to a wooden cabinet by the door. 'Still dosing yourself with that home brewed fire water?'

Dorita cackled delightfully as she poured a glass of deep red liquor for them both. 'Beats any doctor.' She put the stopper back in the bottle and closed the cabinet door. 'Never did like doctors, anyhow,' she mused as she handed Lovell his drink. 'You know, my grandmother remembers the time when they operated on you with a knife.'

Lovell almost choked on his drink. Did she say grandmother? 'Huh?'

'I know!' concurred the old woman. 'A knife! Can you imagine that?'

Lovell swirled his drink around his glass. It had a sweetness about it that was immediately familiar, but it sure had a kick too. Lifting his gaze, he realised that Dorita was looking at him strangely.

'Tell me about the mission,' she said, at last, gesturing to him to join her at the table.

Lovell was amazed. *How the hell did she know about that?* 'It's a toughie,' he admitted.

Dorita reached across and patted his knee. 'Well, I hope they're paying you good,' she smiled.

'Why else would I be doing it?' The captain felt suddenly under scrutiny. Like most Drifters, he knew that Dorita had been born with the power of Extra Sensory Perception.

'How much?' she winked.

'Enough.'

Dorita glanced at him knowingly, then grinned. 'What do you need?'

Lovell set his drink down on the table and wiped his lips. 'I need a way of - '

'Taking a look inside the fortress,' the old woman interrupted, nodding in understanding.

Lovell shook his head in wonder. 'You've gotten good at that, Dorita.'

As if in response, Dorita downed the last of her drink, inhaled deeply, then stared with blank, unseeing eyes. 'I see rocks,' she intoned. 'Black, steep, rising to a wall.'

Lovell watched the old woman carefully. 'What's inside?' he asked.

'Inside?' Dorita blinked, snapping out of her trance-like state. 'Your destiny,' she concluded, cryptically.

'Okay,' breathed Lovell. 'That's sure helpful.'

Dorita chuckled as she walked stiffly to another curtain strung over a doorway. 'I'm getting old. You need my great-grandson.' Beckoning Lovell to follow her, she swept the curtain aside and stepped through into the room beyond.

Following her, Lovell found himself in a smaller cabin lined with shelves of books, bric-a-brac, and antiques. A young boy sat cross-legged by a glowing brazier, a pile of scrap metal on the floor. As Lovell watched, he saw the lad was building some kind of model robot from the lengths of metal and wire beside him.

'He's a smart kid,' said Dorita proudly as the boy looked up. He didn't seem particularly interested in the newcomer by the woman's side. 'Jhy? This is Lovell.'

Jhy gave a sniff of indifference before applying himself to his task.

'Say hello, Jhy.'

The boy deigned to look up again. 'Hello Jhy,' he said with a cheeky grin.

Dorita rolled her eyes as Lovell smiled back. 'Hi.'

'Mr Lovell would like to see Dash.'

Lovell looked surprised. 'I would?' He felt Dorita dig him in the ribs. 'I mean, yeah, sure. I would.'

Immersed in his hobby, Jhy didn't move.

'Well, go get him!' Dorita commanded. Making a big show of having been interrupted, the boy stopped what he was doing, rose to his feet and slouched off to a shelving unit in the corner of the room.

'He needs plenty of affection,' said Dorita beneath her breath.

After a moment, Jhy returned holding a metal unit on four slender legs. A head had been placed on the main structure with beady sensors for eyes, antennae for whiskers and triangular audio receptor units for ears. Jhy set the strange object on the threadbare carpet by his feet.

'Mr Lovell may want to use Dash,' Dorita explained. The boy looked as disinterested as ever. 'He's paying in gold.' Suddenly, Jhy brightened up considerably.

'How much?' he squealed, clapping his hands together in excitement.

Caught off guard, Lovell thought on his feet. 'We'll talk about that later,' he flustered, casting a look of accusation at Dorita.

'Want to see what he can do?' Jhy's eyes were wide with excitement. It was amazing what the promise of payment could do, thought Lovell, wryly.

'Sure,' he grunted.

Bending down to press a switch on the metal box by his feet, Jhy ran off to hide among a pile of junk in a darker corner of the room. After a moment's silence, he called to his creation. 'Here, Dash! Here, boy!'

As Lovell looked on, he saw the metal box on the floor spring to life. Lights burned behind its eyes and its whiskers twitched. Springing to its feet and giving a mechanical yelp of delight, the metal dog bounded off across the room in search of its master. A few minutes later, and Jhy was standing at Lovell's feet, his robot pet in his arms.

'See?' the boy asked, excitedly. 'He found me!'

Lovell was distinctly unimpressed. 'Yeah, nice,' he nodded. 'Very good.'

'So,' panted Jhy, 'what's the job?'

Lovell sighed and dropped to his haunches. 'Look, kid,' he began, resting a hand on the boy's shoulder, 'I don't think - '

'Tell him,' Dorita interrupted, her manner suddenly brusque.

Lovell relented. 'Okay. It's an undercover surveillance. But listen, a mechanical dog isn't - ' Again, he felt Dorita nudge him in the ribs. Turning to look at the old woman, he saw she was standing with a finger on her lips. She nodded towards Jhy. Looking back to the boy, Lovell saw he was standing with his eyes tightly closed. Suddenly, without a word of command, Dash bounded away.

All was quiet on board the freighter. Clarence dozed on the low sofa as Sumara sat cross-legged in a position of meditation. Over by the table, Rudy was trying to refine his manual dexterity. Reaching out, he closed his fingers gingerly around a coffee cup. A second passed. Rudy's eyes flashed with pride as he plucked the cup from the table. Instantly, it crumpled in his grasp. Smashing his fist against the table with frustration, Rudy rested his heavy head in a metal hand, despondent again.

Clarence stretched on the sofa, the noise rousing him from a restful sleep. 'Remind me never to ask you for a head massage,' he teased as he swung his legs to the floor. 'Hang on, what was that?'

Trying to follow his gaze, Rudy's head swivelled around a hundred and eighty degrees. 'Where?'

'Right there.' Clarence rose and loped to the living quarters' window. Peering through the glass, he could see nothing but the string of Drifters' vehicles outside. 'I thought I saw...' he scratched his chest as he thought.

'What is it, Clarence?' Rudy had lumbered to the window to investigate.

'Ah, nothing,' Clarence said finally, heading back to the sofa. 'Forget it.'

As the chimpanzee settled himself down to sleep once more, Rudy returned to the coffee cups on the table. This time, he'd get it right.

'One of them's an ape.' Jhy still had his eyes tight shut as he described the scene. 'There's a robot, and the other man's sitting sort of half asleep.'

Lovell's mouth hung open. 'What does he look like?'

'No hair,' Jhy replied in his trance. 'He's wearing a funny robe. The ape's called Clarence.'

Lovell had heard enough. 'Okay,' he relented, 'that's impressive. But, how?'

'Dash is watching them,' Jhy explained, simply. 'I sent him to your ship.'

'He's inside my ship?' Lovell was aghast. How many times had he told Clarence to seal the hatch when he was gone?

Jhy shook his head and laughed. 'No. He's out in space looking through the window.'

Lovell thought for a moment. 'Call him back.'

Jhy shrugged and called aloud. 'Here, Dash!'

No sooner had Jhy's mouth closed than Lovell was in the corridor, running at some speed back to the airlock. Just as he reached the gaudy picture on the wall, he heard the airlock hiss open ahead of him. Suddenly, Dash was bounding past him, eager to get back to his master. Coming to a swift halt, Lovell turned on his heels. By the time he reached Dorita's room, Dash was in Jhy's arms. Lovell leaned against the door frame to catch his breath.

'ESP?' he gasped, clutching at his heaving chest.

'Jhy can see what Dash sees,' said Dorita with more than a hint of pride. 'He hears what Dash hears.' She tousled the boy's hair in a display of affection. 'I told you he was a smart kid.'

XI

THE CALM BEFORE THE STORM

Jhy sat cradling Dash on his lap as he looked around him. Now he got to see the freighter's crew with his own eyes. If he craned his neck from his seat in the living quarters, he could see Lovell and Clarence on the flight deck. He kept noticing the chimp looking back at him. Sizing him up. Directly opposite the boy, the strange mystic was giving the huge robot a lesson in controlling his grip. Of all his new crewmates, Rudy was the one who perplexed Jhy the most. It was hard to develop a psychic link with robots. He had only managed it with Dash because he had built him with his own hands. For now, Rudy remained unreadable, and that troubled Jhy.

Sumara was holding out a small, white feather. 'A delicate, fragile fragment of nature,' he intoned, gently. Rudy's attention was riveted. 'Take it.'

The great metal monster recoiled. 'I couldn't,' he gasped. 'I'd break it.'

Sumara's voice was suddenly firmer. 'Take it. Concentrate your mind on its fragility.'

Rudy seemed to take a breath to steady his nerves, then his huge fingers closed around the feather. Slowly, he held it up before him.

'Now,' instructed Sumara, his voice more gentle. 'Let it fall.'

Rudy's eyes blazed with the concentration. Jhy was sure he could hear the whirring of tiny fans from somewhere within the robot's mechanisms. He was clearly working hard. Holding the rest of his body in perfect stillness, Rudy uncoiled his fingers and let the feather go, watching it as it floated to the floor.

Sumara smiled. 'You see?'

The giant robot stared down at the feather, enrapt. 'It didn't break!' he whispered. Then, much louder, 'I did it!'

The mystic nodded, wisely. 'All journeys, however long, must start with a single step.'

Having seen enough, Jhy joined Clarence and Lovell on the flight deck.

'I want to talk to you, Lovell,' he said, boldly.

'About what?' Lovell swung round to face him, but not before casting a glance to his hairy companion. Clarence leaned closer in to listen.

'Our fee.'

Clarence tried hard to suppress a snigger.

'*Our* fee?' Lovell echoed.

Jhy nodded down to Dash. The robot dog was nestled in his arms, his whisker antennae twitching. 'For me and Dash.'

'Kid,' Lovell sighed, 'he's just a robot. You don't see me paying no fee to Rudy.' He strained to see through to the living quarters, checking Rudy hadn't heard.

'Dash is special,' Jhy pleaded.

Lovell could see he wasn't backing down. 'Okay, I'll be right with you.'

Seemingly satisfied with the response, Jhy clutched Dash closer to his chest and walked back towards the living quarters.

'Well,' sighed Clarence as he reached for his coffee. 'The team's complete.'

Lovell scratched the stubble on his chin. 'Yeah, all we needed was a smart ass kid.'

Night was closing in. The five moons had risen over Kestra, and Estoran's mountains loomed up into the darkness around the city. The valley between them was a cradle of light. Brightly lit towers pierced the sky and the headlamps of flying vehicles picked out the traffic lanes that wound around them.

Colonel Zana sat alone in the War Room of the Kestran Intelligence Bureau. Moving to the central table, she stabbed at a button to reveal the model of the formidable Zargon fortress. As she peered closer at the stronghold's fortifications, it seemed even more impregnable than before. She was so enrapt in the model that she barely heard the hiss of the door opening behind her.

'I've got my team,' came a voice.

Zana spun round, her almond eyes wide. There stood John D. Lovell. He held a data tablet in front of him, a list of names and pictures displayed on the screen. Zana took them without a word, the faintest of smiles playing on her lips.

'A mystic monk, a wrecking ball on legs and a kid with a pet dog. Way to go.'

'I'd vouch for them all.' Lovell snatched the tablet back. 'We're ready.'

Zana nodded. 'There's just one more thing, Captain Lovell.'

'Oh, what's that?' Lovell swept his hat from his head as Zana moved to the door behind him.

'Dinner,' she replied.

Open to the night sky, the restaurant was a popular location with romantics and dreamers. The stars and moons in the heavens danced in the ripples of the lake, its inky black waters hemmed in on all sides by the brooding mountains. Here and there, small fires burned on floating platforms, lighting the way for the lily pads that drifted lazily upon the surface. A water plant with multi-coloured lantern-shaped flowers glowed in beautiful pastel colours from the banks. Shimmering flower lanterns drooped from large reed beds that floated freely about the lake.

Lovell felt distinctly underdressed. Sitting bolt upright in the artificial water lily that had been designated as their dining pod, he could see that those around him were dressed for the kill. He smoothed his crumpled shirt in an effort to fit in with the sophisticated crowd around him. He was fooling no one. Opposite him, sipping daintily from a long-stemmed glass, Colonel Zana sat in her uniform. In a concession to the informality of the evening, she had undone a single button on her collar.

'That was great,' enthused Lovell as he finished his meal. Zana didn't have the heart to tell him most of it was still left between his teeth.

'Lanta eggs,' replied the Colonel with a smile.

Lovell grimaced as he swallowed his final mouthful. 'Must've been the sauce that made the difference,' he said. Swinging his table away from him, he leaned back in the plush cushions that filled the lily pad.

'This sure is something special,' he sighed. Zana nodded as she looked around at the other floating pods. Couples smooched together as they shared their meals, more interested in each other than in their food. 'Which makes me wonder just what you want.'

Zana did her best to look hurt. 'Want?'

'Come on Zana, I know when I'm being wined and dined. What are you after?'

The Colonel pushed her table away and sat back, drink in hand. 'You're the wild card in this operation, Lovell. I want to know more about you.'

'Such as?' Lovell reached for a beer.

'Why did you resign?'

There was a long, uneasy pause. Lovell took a swig. 'Resign?'

'From the Star Fleet.'

'Isn't it in my record?' he asked, affecting innocence.

Zana leaned forward probing his eyes with her own. 'Not the reasons.'

Lovell crunched the empty beer can up in a fist and threw it to the floor. 'I was married.' He gazed out at the ripples on the water and dropped a hand over the side of the lily pad. It felt cool and fresh. 'My wife was killed,' he explained quietly.

'Space accident. It seemed a good time to make a new start. He flicked his eyes towards Zana to see her sitting, enrapt at his tale. 'So, here I am.'

Zana couldn't take her almond eyes off him. 'I'm sorry,' she said, sadly.

Lovell waved a hand. 'It was a long time ago.'

'Maybe,' said Zana, quietly. 'But I'm still sorry.'

'For what?'

Zana held his gaze. 'For digging too deep.'

Reaching out, Lovell patted her hand. 'No problem. If you're sending a man on a mission like this, I 'spose you gotta know what makes him tick.'

Zana laughed at this, removing her hand a little quicker than Lovell would have liked. 'Oh, I know what makes you tick, all right. You've got a million of them in your hold.'

Lovell shrugged. 'That certainly helps,' he agreed. 'But there's more to it than that. I try to be the kind of man she would have wanted me to be.' He gave a wry smile. 'Most of the time I fail. Miserably. But, that doesn't stop me trying.'

'And what would she want of you now, John D. Lovell?' Zana was settling back in her cushions.

'Well, mostly,' the captain grinned, 'she'd want me back in one piece.'

Zana nodded, draping her hand lazily over the side of the pod. 'Then make sure you do that for her, Lovell. And the next meal will be on you.'

XII

RED-HANDED

The Zargon fortress sat brooding in the darkness. Light itself had been banished from the asteroid, to be replaced by a cruel, cold black. The inhospitable landscape that surrounded the tall column of rock on which the stronghold was nestled, offered nothing but bleak oblivion. At the base of the tower, the bleached bones of unfortunate soldiers lay blasted by the unforgiving interstellar radiation

Inside the stronghold, Leutna Braxx walked swiftly down a corridor, a piece of paper clutched in his hand. He was travelling at such a pace that a sheen of sweat had appeared on his forehead. Reaching the central control room, he acknowledged the salutes of two Zargon guards and pressed the panel for entry. He settled his breathing as the door swung open with a hiss.

Grand Leutna Gahn stood by an observation window, gazing out onto the asteroid below. Gahn turned to watch Braxx approach over the gantry from the main door. Looking down, the Leutna could see rows of operatives sat at banks of computers, each of them absorbed by the task in hand.

'There's something quite inspiring about this view,' the Grand Leutna enthused as Braxx came to his side. 'It's the very absence of life that I find so beguiling.' Gahn was flexing his baton in his hands as he spoke. 'They say where there is life, there is hope,' he smiled. 'But hope is a dangerous thing, is it not, Leutna Braxx?'

Braxx snapped to attention. 'Yes, sir,' he agreed. In truth, he was keen to deliver his message as fast as he could then return to his business.

'I have no doubt the Kestrans are full of hope,' Gahn was musing aloud. 'But hope deceives. It leads you astray. It prolongs the agony.' There was a silence while Gahn contemplated his own words. Braxx cleared his throat. 'Intelligence report, sir,' he announced, holding up the readout before him. 'From our agent on Kestra.'

The Grand Leutna seemed irritated at the interruption. Snatching the piece of paper from Braxx, he gestured that the Leutna should stand a little further back as he read. Slowly, as his eyes scanned the page, he broke into a malicious smile.

'What action are we taking?' Gahn asked as he handed the paper back.

'A simple space-jack, sir,' Braxx replied, watching for the Grand Leutna's reaction.

Gahn nodded, satisfied. 'Excellent,' he sneered.

Lovell cast a final look around the living quarters. Sumara, Jhy and Rudy sat in their take-off positions. Nestling in a corner of the flight deck, he could see the assembled paraphernalia and equipment they would use on their mission. Coils of rope lay on the floor next to clamps and torches.

'It's a long ride,' the captain rasped. 'I suggest you all get some rest when you can.' Looking at his assembled team, Lovell felt a pang of doubt. They were about to be tested and he wasn't a hundred per cent sure they'd not be found wanting. His eyes flicked to Jhy, suddenly remembering the kid could read minds. Jhy stared back, his face blank. Perhaps he was too young, thought Lovell hopefully, and he flashed his best smile of reassurance.

Easing himself through the door to the flight deck, Lovell flung himself on his chair. 'Let's go,' he said with a look to Clarence. Already buckled up, the chimpanzee reached forward to the controls. There was a whine of turbines from the rear of the ship and a kick of thrust jolted the cockpit.

'Steady now,' soothed Clarence as if he were talking to a restless child, and suddenly the engines burst into life. Lovell saw the space port drop away from them as the freighter rattled its way through the Kestran atmosphere. Somewhere behind him, something fell over.

As they entered smoother space, Lovell released his restraints and made for the door. 'I'm just gonna check we've got everything we need for the mission,' he called back to Clarence as he left the flight deck.

'Sure,' called Clarence after him. 'And maybe pick up whatever fell over when we launched.'

The living quarters were quiet. Sumara was sat cross-legged on a bunk in silent meditation. Jhy was playing fetch with his robot dog, throwing a monkey wrench repeatedly into a corner, only for Dash to spring off excitedly to retrieve it each time.

'Cute,' muttered Lovell, unconvincingly. He waved at Rudy to get his attention, then gestured that the robot should accompany him to the hold. Lifting himself from a chair with a huge effort, Rudy lumbered after him to the rear of the ship.

'When we land, I want you to take this out on the surface.' Lovell was pulling a container out from under a dirty tarpaulin as he spoke, looking around him to check that only Rudy had seen.

'Out on the surface,' Rudy boomed in acknowledgement.

'Keep your voice down!' Lovell glared at the great mechanical beast before him, then turned to the container and flipped open the lid. Even in the subdued light of the cargo hold, the gold cast a glow on the surrounding metalwork. Again, Lovell glanced back to make sure no one else was nearby.

'Now,' he whispered, 'when you get it outside, you look around for someplace to hide it.' He stopped suddenly, aware he was being watched. Jhy's robot dog was sitting at his feet, his whiskers twitching. And Lovell knew what that meant. 'How long have you been there?' he asked, the implications becoming clear. He turned to Rudy. 'How long has *that* been there?'

Neither Dash nor Rudy responded. But then, they didn't have to. There, in the doorway to the hold, stood Jhy, his arms folded in expectation of an explanation.

'Alright, kid,' Lovell relented. 'Let's talk.'

'About what?' Jhy responded in mock innocence. He called to his robot and Dash bounced up to his young Master's side.

'Don't get clever with me, kid. You see what he sees.' He pointed at Dash, then sat on the container beside him. 'How much?'

Jhy smiled.

'Your fee,' Lovell said, resigned. 'How much?'

'A quarter share,' said Jhy, daringly.

Lovell sprang to his feet, aghast at the sum. 'A *what*?'

'Two hundred thousand for me,' Jhy clarified helpfully, 'fifty thousand for Dash. A quarter of a million.' He bent down to scoop his pet into his arms. Lovell was sure the thing's eyes were glowing just that little bit brighter.

'If you think I'm paying that useless hunk of metal a single credit,' he began, 'you can go take a - '

'*This* useless hunk of metal would also like a share,' came a voice behind him. Rudy had stretched himself up to his full, intimidating height.

Lovell could scarcely believe his eyes. 'You?' he bawled. 'You're a machine! What good is money to you? You don't need money.'

'There is something,' Rudy replied calmly, his great head inclined to the floor. 'Something I wish to buy.' He lifted his gaze to meet Lovell's. 'I wish to buy my freedom.'

Not for the first time in the past few days, Lovell's mouth hung open. 'Freedom?'

Rudy nodded, the servos in his neck whining as he leaned forward to explain. 'Yes. Buy my freedom and serve you. Sir.'

Lovell was lost for words. At the doorway, Jhy stamped his foot to get the captain's attention. 'Do Rudy and I have a deal?' It was more a demand than a question.

Lovell sighed and pinched at the bridge of his nose. He didn't seem to have much choice. 'Alright,' he said at last. 'I'll think about it.'

XIII

SPACE-JACK

Flight 128 was ahead of schedule. The Star Liner had made good time as it sped, dart-like, between Kestra and Vega. Inside, an assortment of passengers listened gratefully as the pilot notified them via the intercom of their intended early arrival. As the speakers clicked off, the chatter of excited voices filled the cabin. In Economy Class, a family of holidaymakers busied themselves with their customs forms. In Business Class, a smartly dressed man snapped off his comms and settled back in his seat for a quick doze. In First Class, Colonel Zana was thinking of Lovell. She had never put all her hopes in one man before. She knew he'd be on his way by now. She wasn't a superstitious person, nevertheless as she gazed out through the windows at the stars beyond, she wondered if she should wish upon one of them.

'And the second meeting is at Fourteen Hundred Hours.'

Zana turned to the Intelligence Captain beside her. 'I'm sorry,' she said. 'Miles away.'

Captain Thawn shut the folder on his lap with a friendly smile. 'It's all right, Colonel Zana. We'll go through this in detail when we arrive.'

Zana nodded in thanks.

'Would you like another drink?'

'That would be lovely,' Zana smiled. 'Thank you.'

The stewardess was busy serving drinks to the rear when she heard the ping of the bell. Looking down the aisle towards First Class, the small Heads Up Display in her glasses saw through the dividing bulkhead and illuminated seat number thirty-four. Scrolling text beside the seat told her that the passenger in question required a Zinca Juice. Acknowledging the summons with a tap of her glasses, she looked down at the two passengers next to her to complete their order first. She was just in time to see one of them, a squat looking man with a thick neck, reaching for her throat.

Before she had the time to cry out, the man had got behind her and swung his arm around her neck. Barely able to breathe, the stewardess watched as the man's companion, a taller figure with long hair, jumped into the aisle. To her horror, she saw that he was carrying a gun. Her vision faded to black as she kicked out uselessly into the air.

The squat man dragged the unconscious stewardess back to a passenger toilet cubicle. Pushing at the door, he propped her up against the washstand, locked her inside then sprinted up the aisle to join his companion. Several passengers had noticed the commotion by now, and the faint chatter of passengers in flight was turning to something more shrill.

Pulling at the curtain, the two men barged into First Class, both holding their guns in the air. 'Everyone stay calm!' the tall man shouted, 'and I'll have no cause to use these!' He lifted his shirt to reveal several Light Grenades hanging from his belt.

Zana looked round, shocked by the intrusion. Her military background enabled her to evaluate the situation at once. 'It's a space-jack,' she gasped. She began running through the potential consequences in her head.

'I know,' came a calm voice from beside her. She felt a pressure at her thigh. Looking down, she saw that the Captain was pressing a small handgun to her leg. Her almond eyes gazed in horror as the truth hit home. 'You're part of it?'

Captain Thawn nodded slowly, a rueful smile on his face. 'Oh, don't look so surprised, Colonel,' he said, his voice adopting a strange sing-song tone. 'The Zargons are winning this war. I've just chosen my side a little earlier than everyone else.'

'Do we know what it is?'

Grand Leutna Gahn stared down at the monitor. An illuminated trace made its way across the screen. A small craft was entering the asteroid's orbital path.

'A B156 Transporter, sir,' replied Braxx.

Gahn smiled. 'A B156? I didn't realise any of those heaps were still flying.'

'It's barely flying, sir,' said Braxx, daring to share the joke. 'Our sensors indicate it's unarmed. I can't see that it poses any possible threat.'

The Grand Leutna flexed the baton with his hands, his cold eyes fixed on the screen. Braxx could tell he was grinding his teeth. 'Navigational error?'

Braxx nodded. 'Could be, sir.'

'The pilot's probably as decrepit as his ship.' Gahn chuckled, darkly.

Lovell's freighter skimmed low over the surface of the asteroid. As Clarence piloted the craft, Lovell was checking their position.

'We're coming up to the touchdown area,' he said, pointing through the windshield. 'There!' He turned to his co-pilot. 'Take her down.'

Clarence eased the controls forward and reduced speed. Soon they were rounding a large rocky outcrop before dropping to the plain behind it. With a hiss of vector thrusters, the freighter began its descent. Clarence guided the craft expertly down to land on the flat plain beyond the escarpment. There was a jolt as she came to rest.

'Nicely done,' said Lovell as he released his straps and made for the doorway to the living quarters. Sumara, Jhy and Rudy were tensed for action. 'The asteroid is seven hours through an eight hour day. Rest for an hour. We'll move out as soon as it's dark.'

'It's gone down in the rock field.'

Leutna Braxx had followed Gahn down a flight of metal stairs to the computer room below. They had stood and watched as an operative tracked the craft in its descent to the asteroid.

'Crashed?' asked the Grand Leutna, gnawing at his lip. This didn't feel right at all.

The computer operator glanced back. 'Possibly.'

Gahn considered a moment, then turned to Braxx. 'Check it out. Send a patrol.'

Leutna Braxx saluted. 'Yes, sir.'

Beyond the horizon, barely a mile away, a ramp had extended from the freighter to the barren ground below. Lovell and his team had assembled by the exit.

Lovell took a deep breath. 'This artificial atmosphere smells like home.'

'Remind me not to come calling.' Clarence wrinkled his nose.

Lovell turned to Rudy as he stepped out onto the ramp. 'Give us two hours,' he murmured. 'Any longer and the radiation'll get us.'

Rudy nodded. 'I understand. May I wish you good luck, sir?'

The captain looked around him. 'Let's go.' Carrying two large packs and an impressive looking laser gun on a sling, Lovell stepped out onto the asteroid.

Jhy reached up to adjust the straps on the small packs on his back. He followed Lovell a few steps down the ramp, then turned to whistle for Dash. The diminutive robot jumped eagerly from the craft to follow his master down to the surface.

Following close behind, Clarence brandished a laser rifle in one hairy hand and a small pack in the other. Sumara came last of all, unarmed and looking as serene as ever.

As he reached the bottom of the ramp, Lovell stood aside to let his companions pass. He looked back at his ship. She had never been a looker, he thought as his eyes ranged over her distinctive hammerhead design. But, right now, he would give anything to know for sure he'd see her again.

Soon, Lovell was leading the motley group along a rocky gully some way from the freighter. Sumara brought up the rear. Clarence, glancing round to him from time to time, noticed that he left no footprints as he walked. Suddenly Jhy, from his position in the line behind Lovell, held up his hand. 'Wait.'

Lovell turned as they came to a halt. 'What is it?'

Jhy pointed down at Dash, standing alert at his feet. His ears were pricked, his whiskers quivering. 'He can hear something.'

Lovell strained his ears but could hear only silence.

Jhy was bending down to Dash. 'What is it, Dash? Go find it, boy!'

As the robot dog bounded off into the darkness, Jhy screwed his eyes up tight, just as Lovell had seen him do in his Drifter caravan. Enthralled, Clarence and Sumara leaned in to watch.

'It's a patrol,' Jhy gasped, suddenly. 'Headed this way.'

Lovell looked around. 'Take cover!' he barked

The group spread out at once and hid among the rocks. As Dash ran back to Jhy's arms, the boy carried him to safety behind a crystalline formation. In mere moments they were all entirely hidden. Dash poked his nose from behind the rock as Jhy closed his eyes again. Through his dog's visual circuits, he could see the group of Zargon soldiers making their way over the rocks. Their leader crouched low as he walked, his gun held to his shoulder. Three more followed in a fan formation, each of them sweeping the area with their weapons. Their sleek black uniforms seemed to glisten in the starlight. Soon, they were within two feet of the boy. Jhy held his breath and concentrated hard, determined not to break the psychic link with his robot.

Behind the soldiers, Lovell pressed himself against a column formation, careful not to move a muscle. He looked around for Clarence, only to see the chimp winking back from inside a small gully. Lovell raised an eyebrow, directing Clarence's gaze down to his gun as he subtly squeezed the trigger. *Should we spring them?* he seemed to say. Clarence shook his head. *Not now.* Beyond the gully, Sumara seemed to have become at one with the rock around him. Lovell squinted as he tried to pick him out, convinced that even his skin colour had changed to better blend in with his surroundings.

The patrol safely past, Jhy broke his connection with Dash and stepped forward to wave the all clear. As the group inched slowly onwards, the fortress loomed large before them. Jhy looked up in awe at the forbidding sheer rock face. As the motley group assembled around him, Sumara put a hand gently on the boy's shoulder. The mystic smiled down at the boy, nodding in encouragement.

'You think we can make it?' Clarence was asking Lovell.

'It's the only way up,' sighed Lovell as he uncoiled a length of rope from Jhy's shoulders. 'Anyway, what are you worried about?'

Clarence shook his head as he swung his pack from his back. 'My distant forefathers may have swung around in trees, but I get vertigo four feet up.'

'Great,' Lovell breathed in exasperation. 'We've found the only ape who's afraid of heights.'

'It is merely a question of conquering a primitive fear with a strong mind,' added Sumara as he stepped forward to grab the rope.

'Hey!' Clarence protested. 'Who are you calling primitive?'

'Height is of no consequence.' Sumara was attaching himself to the rope in preparation for the climb. 'A man is still the same man even a thousand feet in the air. The perception is all.'

'Oh, yeah?' laughed Clarence as he hooked himself onto the line. 'Then why are you bothering with the rope?'

Sumara gave a smile to show he wasn't taking himself entirely seriously. 'The climb is of no concern to me. The fall, however…' he twinkled.

'I don't need a rope,' Jhy suddenly asserted.

Lovell squatted next to him. 'Put it on, Jhy.'

'I don't need it,' the boy repeated, adamant.

'It's not for you,' Lovell said quietly as he lifted a harness over the boy's head. 'It's for Dorita.' He attached the rope to a clip and ruffled the boy's hair.

Snapping at the cable to see everyone was safely attached, Lovell walked to the base of the tower and looked up. 'Okay, here's what I see,' he began. 'The first fifty feet are pretty smooth. We'll have to cut footholds.'

'We have no time, Lovell,' Clarence warned.

'Allow me, John Lovell.' Sumara pushed his way forward and stood before the sheer cliff before them. Pressing his palms together as if in prayer, he began to sway gently from foot to foot. Lovell squinted as his eyes began to fill with rock dust. Wiping his face, he looked up to see the rock was crumbling. The whole group looked on in amazement as, within moments, handholds started appearing in the smooth rock. Lovell smiled. The climb had begun.

XIV

THE ASCENT

Rudy tried again. The stack of plastic cartons was arranged on the table as a pyramid; evidence of the robot's continued attempts to finesse his grip. Reaching out for the final carton, he closed his metal fingers around it, careful not to squeeze too hard. Keeping the rest of his body still, he swung his great arm across the table to place the carton in its place on top of the tower. His shoulders were bunched in concentration and his eyes glowed with a steady, unwavering light. Suddenly, his aural sensors picked up a noise from outside the ship. Distracted, Rudy lurched forward, his huge arm ploughing through the pyramid on the table. The whole construction crumpled before him. Looking at the carton in his hand he saw that, due to his lapse in concentration, he had crushed it between his heavy fingers. Cursing to himself, he lumbered to the cockpit windshield to investigate just where the noise had come from. Standing stock still for moment, he scanned the rocky plain outside. Nothing. Confident he had been mistaken, he turned back to the table with a mechanical shrug and started the tower all over again.

Roped together, the intrepid band had made good progress up the rock face. Beyond the smooth base of the column, the rock had become more easily traversed. The pitted surface was perfect for climbing, providing many hand and footholds to grab or perch upon to rest. Of all of them, thought Lovell, Dash was having the most fun. Like any dog, he would race ahead then balance precariously on a ledge waiting for his master to catch up. He had the advantage of not having to make contact with the rock at all. During his construction, Jhy had thoughtfully provided the dog with mini thrusters that enabled him to jet here and there whatever the surface.

'We're making good time,' called Lovell as he grabbed at a hold. 'How d'you feel, Clarence?'

The chimp hugged the rock, not daring to look down. 'I think the word is nauseous.'

Just as Lovell was about to respond with another sarcastic comment, he noticed Dash, standing on a rock above them. His whiskers twitched with agitation as he emitted a series of mechanical yelps.

'Kid!' Lovell called to Jhy. 'What's wrong with your dog?'

Jhy looked up. 'He senses danger.'

'Great,' sighed Clarence.

'What sort of danger?' Lovell was looking around him, suddenly fearful.

'I don't know,' the boy admitted. 'But it's close.'

As Lovell clutched at the rock, he felt a tremor in the cliff face. A deep, rumbling throb filled the air.

'What the - '

'I would suggest we hang on tight,' came Sumara's calming voice.

'D'you think?' Clarence replied, pressing his body against the sheer rock face. Above them, an enormous slab of rock was opening in the mountainside. As it pivoted down to a sort of ramp, a spill of light from the fortress' interior flooded the night. To Lovell and his gang below the ramp, it appeared as an enormous rectangular slab impeding their progress.

'What's happening?' roared Clarence above the noise of massive machinery.

'Just hold on!' Lovell cautioned.

'The thought had occurred to me,' the chimp sneered

With the rock door lowered into position, the reason for its opening became apparent. Looking up, Lovell could see a

Space Liner approaching like a dart through the night. With a roar of its engines, it levelled off. Its speed decreased until it dropped gently onto the platform and taxied inside. The great slab of rock began to close, the shaft of light receding until it disappeared completely. The throbbing of machinery ceased. There was an eerie silence.

'Some kind of landing platform,' Lovell called to his companions. 'It must be three hundred feet high.' They hauled themselves onto a ledge and stood looking up.

'Yeah, and it's right in our line of ascent.' Clarence looked despondent.

'That which cannot be crossed must be circumvented,' offered Sumara, barely holding on at all.

'He means we have to go around it,' Clarence explained off Lovell's look of confusion.

The captain shook his head. 'There isn't time,' he grimaced.

'Well,' cautioned the ape, 'if we get caught on that thing when it opens…' He didn't want to think of the implications.

'Yeah,' agreed Lovell. For one moment, Clarence thought he was considering turning back. 'So let's not waste more time talking about it.'

Holding tight to their ropes, the group took a collective breath to steel themselves, then continued their ascent.

With the Space Liner safely docked in the hangar, Colonel Zana found herself singled out from among the other passengers, then force-marched along one of the internal corridors of the stronghold. She was flanked at every step by a duo of brutally-faced Zargon guards who held her by the arms. The little party paused at the end of the corridor for a door to swing open, and Zana found herself face to face with Grand Leutna Gahn.

'My dear Colonel,' he leered. 'Do come in.'

With a sudden movement of her arms, Zana broke free of the guards. Giving them a withering look, she made great play of stepping through the door unaccompanied. It was, by

Zargon standards at least, an opulent room, but its black and silver decor gave it a hard, steely atmosphere. She guessed she must be in the Grand Leutna's private quarters.

'Welcome,' Gahn smiled with an attempted show of civility.

Colonel Zana wasn't falling for it for a moment. 'I demand to be released,' she snapped. 'Immediately.'

The Grand Leutna gestured to two chairs he had had arranged by an observation window. They afforded breath-taking views over the asteroid. 'Demand?' he teased. 'Released? We are not at war.'

He sat back and gestured again at the opposite seat. Zana refused to sit.

'What do you want?' she hissed.

Gahn smiled again and made steeples with his fingers. 'The answer to an interesting question. What are you planning?'

Zana's eyes narrowed, but she said nothing.

'Your Intelligence Captain has told me all about your War Room,' Grand Leutna Gahn continued, 'and the very impressive model of this fortress. Who would have thought you would one day be standing inside it?' He couldn't resist a chuckle at Zana's expense. 'You weren't thinking of an attack, were you?'

Zana blinked. 'Colonel Zana, Kestran Intelligence Division, service number 304/D/764.'

Gahn grit his teeth. That was clearly all she was planning to say for the duration of the interview.

'Very well,' he growled. 'I shall have to see if I can loosen your tongue.' Flipping open a panel in the arm of his chair, he stabbed at a button. Almost immediately, the door swung open to admit the two sour looking guards who had accompanied Zana from the Space Liner.

'Take her away,' the Grand Leutna commanded. 'Question her *thoroughly*.' With a curt nod, the two guards led the silent Zana away. Gahn stared out the observation window for a moment. His brow furrowed as he reached for his baton from a table. Idly tapping it against his hand, he considered his options. Finally, he punched another button in the arm of his chair.

'Braxx, sir,' came a tinny voice.

'Leutna Braxx, I'm bringing forward the strike.'

'Problems, sir?' came the voice.

Gahn gnawed at his lip. 'No, but why take even the slimmest chance? Launch the Battle Cruisers.'

'Yes, sir.' Braxx acknowledged. 'The missiles will be operable in forty five minutes.'

Gahn released the comm switch. Rising from his chair, he stood at the window to drink in the darkness beyond the glass. 'Well, Colonel Zana,' he brooded, flexing his baton in his hands, 'let's see if you'll talk when Planet Kestra is turned into a ball of boiling vapour.' He was straining every sinew to contain his anger. But still, the baton snapped.

An urgent whooping alert blared out through every corridor. Groups of soldiers ran to their battle-stations. In the gigantic hangar carved out of the rock, the raucous sound of the klaxon was drowned out by an even greater roar. The six mighty Battle Cruisers had started their photon engines.

High up on the outside of the escarpment, Lovell felt the tell-tale vibration through his fingers. Looking up, he saw a familiar crack of light appear in the rock. The platform was opening again. And they were all hanging from it. Swinging round on his rope, he called down to his fellow climbers. 'Make fast wherever you can!'

Clarence looked the most panicked of all as the climbing party began to fasten their ropes to whatever holds they could find. Lovell hammered pitons into the rock in a frantic effort to secure their lines. Dash played around him as he did so, whizzing here and there to chew playfully on the metal rods as they were hammered in. 'Hey, kid!' Lovell shouted down to Jhy. 'Will you get this mutt away from me?' Already, the rock was starting to angle dangerously out over the plain below.

As the platform lowered into position, Lovell could hear the sirens blaring from within.

'Launch minus thirty seconds!' came an announcement over a Tannoy.

'This is going to be interesting,' Clarence shouted above the noise, the note of panic in his voice ringing clear above the din.

The launch platform was now angling down towards the horizontal. The band of climbers clung to the rock for their lives. It was like trying to hold on to a jagged, rocky ceiling. As the platform came to its final position with a jolt, Clarence slipped and lost his grip. As the rest of the group looked on in horror, he started to fall. His portion of the rope whipped through the snap link as it played out fast. Lovell felt helpless as he watched his companion fall, only for the rope to snag fast on a piton. It had been hammered hurriedly into the rock as the platform opened, and now it was taking the chimpanzee's full weight. Lovell scrambled down a few feet to take a closer look.

'It seems to be holding!' Sumara called to Lovell. Lovell looked desperately at his companions, all of them clinging desperately to the underside of the platform like spiders to a web. Clarence was swinging fifteen feet below them with nothing between him and the splintered rocks a thousand feet down at the bottom of the tower. He clutched desperately at his rope as he swung.

'Don't look down!' yelled Lovell as gazed down at the staggering, giddy drop beneath him. Just a few feet away, Jhy was clinging grimly to the rock, a look of sheer terror on his face. 'It's okay, kid,' Lovell soothed. 'I've been in worse fixes than this, and I lived to tell the tale.' The boy nodded.

'Lovell!' Sumara called from his position beneath the platform. 'Look!' Lovell followed his gaze to where the piton was moving slightly as Clarence swung on the end of the rope. It looked far from secure in the narrow cleft in the rock. Too much movement or vibration could shake it loose.

'Keep as still as you can!' Lovell yelled above the increasing noise of photon engines warming up. From inside the giant hanger, a countdown was starting.

'Five.'

'Four.'

'Three.'

'Two.'

'Launch one!'

The rock shook as the first Battle Cruiser roared away with a deafening burst of sound. The second followed immediately, climbing away into the night sky. Beneath the platform, the roar of power and the terrible vibration were almost unbearable. Lovell fought desperately to stop himself falling as the third Battle Cruiser blasted away from the platform, its engines aflame. The noise seemed to split the air.

Finally, the piton broke loose from the rock.

Jhy gave an involuntary scream as Clarence fell away. He chimp's mouth opened in horror as he spun to the ground, his arms and legs flailing about him. With the piton loose, there was nothing to stop his fall.

Except Sumara.

As Clarence hurtled towards the ground, he suddenly felt his fall beginning to slow. Daring to look up at the platform he could see Sumara reaching out into thin air, an unnerving look of calm on his face. The chimp knew at once what he was trying to do. Even from this distance, he could see Sumara's hands closing around an imaginary rope. Clarence could feel his descent slowing. Suddenly, he came to a stop.

'I'm okay!' he called to his companions. Lovell looked on in relief as Sumara held the rope firm in his mind's eye. Finally, Clarence was hanging steady courtesy of the mystic's strong sinewy hands and a psychic grip on the rope.

With all the Battle Cruisers gone, there was a respite from the dreadful din of their engines. Lovell cautioned his companions to hang on as the platform began to move back to the vertical. The crack of light disappearing above them, the raiding party felt a jolt as the platform slid back into its housing. The rock face was dark again, and an eerie silence hung in the air. Finding a sturdy foothold, Lovell joined Sumara and Jhy where they had found a position near Clarence's rope. As they pulled on the line, Lovell noticed that, despite never having touched the rope, Sumara's hands were blistered and burned. Together, they pulled Clarence up the last remaining feet of rock. Soon enough, he was able to find a foothold himself, frantically attaching himself to the more secure pitons as he climbed.

'You're one hell of a guy, Sumara,' the chimpanzee breathed gratefully. He stood beside them at last, his body shaking in a delayed response to his near-death experience. Clarence, too, had noticed Sumara's bloodied hands.

'I will take that as a compliment, Clarence B. Bond,' the mystic responded calmly, closing his eyes. As he sunk into an instant trance state, incredibly, his hands began to heal. As Clarence looked on wide-eyed, the rough and bloodied skin smoothed over. In a matter of moments, the palms of his hands looked as if they had never been injured. 'It was really nothing,' Sumara smiled enigmatically, his eyes snapping open.

Lovell looked at the cliff face above them. 'The going appears relatively easy from here on,' he said, encouragingly. 'Let's get to the top.' As Sumara led the way, Clarence linked himself onto the chain with a new rope. Lovell hung back to talk to Jhy.

'How you doin', kid?' he asked, concerned.

'I'm okay,' Jhy replied, passing one hand over another on the rope.

Lovell nodded. There was something more going on in the boy's mind. 'What are you thinking?'

'I'm thinking I undercharged you.' With that, Jhy set off like a mountain goat, Dash bouncing from ledge to ledge as he climbed. Lovell shook his head and laughed. The kid was clearly hard as nails.

'Battle Fleet launched, Commander.' Braxx's voice sang out loud and clear from the loudspeaker.

Grand Leutna Gahn nodded, satisfied. 'Excellent,' he smiled. 'Start the countdown.'

Punching off the comms, he looked towards the observation window. An image of the six Battle Cruisers had appeared on the glass, their trajectory and technical stats scrolling in a text box beneath them. A digital countdown clock glowed in the bottom right hand corner as he watched, and immediately started to move from forty minutes towards zero. The Grand Leutna bunched his fists. Nothing could stop them now.

XV

THE BERSERKER

Although heavy, the crate of gold was no match for Rudy's brute strength. The grav-lifts had been of little use on the dusty ground of the asteroid, so he had simply ripped them off and hoisted the container onto his broad shoulders. Finding a rocky outcrop that would serve as the perfect marker for future recovery, he used his great hands to dig a deep hole, then deposited the crate inside it. As he smoothed over the arid soil with a foot, he heard three electronic bleeps. He flipped open a small metallic hatch in his arm to see a green light flashing on and off. He snapped the hatch closed. It was time to go. Looking again to be sure the crate was well covered, Rudy committed the location coordinates to his memory banks, then turned his bulk back to the freighter.

Just as he disappeared behind some rocks, the Zargon patrol hove into view. The Patrol Leader was still up front, scanning the way ahead with his rifle. Three more followed, each with their Heat Exchange Guns held high, ready for the chance to use them. As they rounded a particular rock formation, the Patrol Leader called the squad to a halt. He waved his second in command forward and they both crouched down while the remaining soldiers took up defensive positions around them.

'What are we to make of those?' the Patrol Leader asked, pointing to two large indentations in the dust.

'Undoubtedly made by something heavy,' his subordinate replied. 'Footprints?'

The soldiers tensed, holding their HE-Guns at the ready. 'Look around,' the Patrol Leader barked. 'There's bound to be more.'

As the soldiers fanned out, Rudy ran up the ramp into the freighter. His proximity sensors had alerted him to the patrol's position and he knew time was running out. Punching at a button with his great fist, he lumbered onto the flight deck as the ramp retracted. He stabbed at some buttons on a monitor. Soon, the Zargon patrol was visible on the screen. Rudy could see one of the soldiers was poking around the rock pile where he had buried the gold. *Ah well*, he thought, somewhere deep in his positronic brain stem. *They'll soon have distraction enough.*

Standing by the dashboard, he initiated the ignition sequence and listened for the roar of the engines. As they sprung to life, he saw the soldiers on the monitor react at once. Pulling at the control column, he increased power to the engines and engaged the freighter's vertical thrusters. In a matter of moments, the asteroid was dropping away from him. Turning sharply, Rudy flew the vehicle directly over the Zargon patrol. They raised their guns in response, throwing small bursts of flame behind them as they fired. The freighter seemed to ignore the bursts of fire raking its hull. Its engines screaming in complaint, it turned away from the Zargon patrol and climbed towards the fortress on the mountain.

Grand Leutna Gahn and Leutna Braxx were once more in the central control room, hunched over a monitor with its operator. He pointed to indicate the freighter, showing on his screen as a luminous trace.

'It's headed this way,' he said, looking up to the Grand Leutna.

Gahn frowned. 'The pilot must be deranged. Fire warning shots. And put this on a screen somewhere.'

The operative flicked a switch and a screen buzzed to life on the wall before him. It showed the freighter skimming the asteroid's surface at alarming speed. The picture divided in half to show the vehicle's progress on one side and the scramble to get to the laser cannons on the fortress walls on the other. Zargon soldiers hurried to their posts and trained their sights on the marauding freighter as it sped towards them. The cannons recoiled back between each bolt as the lasers lit the night sky. As commanded, their intent was to warn the freighter off its attack, but it soon became apparent that the pilot wasn't listening. As the lasers glanced harmlessly off its hull, it seemed he was more resolute than ever to stay on course.

'It's maintaining course, sir,' the operative reported.

'It's insanity,' breathed Braxx. He could hear the Grand Leutna grinding his teeth beside him.

'Destroy it,' Gahn hissed, then he turned and walked away.

Braxx leaned forward to stab at the comms. 'Control to gun teams,' he barked. 'Fire at will. Fire to destroy.'

Despite the onslaught, the Transporter maintained its level flight, heading straight for the fortress. Raked by the laser fire, great chunks of metal were torn from the hull and spun away.

On the flight deck, Rudy completely disregarded the pounding the ship was being subjected to. Bracing himself against a bulkhead as the freighter was buffeted by gunfire, the huge robot leaned forward over the control column. The fortress loomed large in his windshield. The closer he got, the more violent the onslaught became. Taking it at almost point blank range, the freighter was taking a beating. Alarms sounded and lights flashed from the dashboard but Rudy ignored them all. He knew the ship could make it. Just as he punched a button for a final timed thrust of the engines, the flight deck took a series of direct hits. The windshield was blown in and the cabin was exposed to the open air. As the smoke cleared, the giant robot pushed aside a piece of fallen bulkhead obstructing his view. Still clinging on to what was left of the controls, he fixed his gaze through the yawning gap that was the front of the ship. Raked by the laser fire, it was a miracle the freighter was still in the air. As it neared the fortress walls at breakneck speed, the whole of the rear section was a mass of flames. Peering through the smoke, Rudy could see how close he was. With his enormous reach, he almost thought he could reach out and touch the cannon on the fortress walls. The soldiers were abandoning their posts now, and running for cover as the freighter approached. Rudy was sure he could see the whites of their eyes.

Finally, the ship ploughed into the wall at full throttle, tearing a huge hole in the rock. After a pregnant pause, the fuel tanks exploded. Great mountains of masonry cascaded down, filling the air with dust and smoke. As each fuel cell in turn was compromised, explosion followed explosion, rocking the stronghold and sending the soldiers and operatives fleeing in panic. Finally, an eerie silence descended over the smoking debris. The wall had been breached.

'It was suicide, sir.' Leutna Braxx stood smartly to attention in the Grand Leutna's private quarters.

'What about the crew?' Gahn was at the observation window. He could just make out a smudge of smoke rising in the distance to his right.

Braxx looked doubtful. 'There is no possible chance anyone could have survived.'

Gahn thought long and hard. 'As you say,' he said at last. 'A suicide mission.' Seemingly satisfied with the explanation, he turned his cold eyes onto the Leutna. 'Start repair work at first light.'

XVI

POINT OF ENTRY

The dust had settled over the debris. The great scar in the fortress walls had produced huge cracks in the surrounding bulwarks. As a Zargon sentry looked on, teams of fire-fighters wound up their hoses. Huge water containers were dragged away on their grav-lifts, the fires, at last, extinguished. Looking over the precipice, the sentry could see that the bulk of the freighter had fallen to the rocks below. The distinctive hammerhead, however, remained embedded in the wall, its exposed circuitry sparking in the damp air. The area cleared and contained, the sentry moved back to his position on the wall. Fortunately, as he passed a large piece of brickwork dislodged by the impact, he was looking the other way. Had he happened to glance back, he would have noticed a small head appearing from behind the brick.

His ears pricked, Dash watched as the sentry passed. Beyond the wall, on a ledge of rock, Jhy had his eyes squeezed shut.

'It's clear,' he whispered.

Crouched beside him, Sumara nodded, a look of serene calm on his face. Moving silently forward through the gaping hole in the wall, the mystic paused to focus on the sentry. The Zargon guard was half turning, as if he sensed something or someone behind him. But it was too late. As if from nowhere, a crushing blow landed on his neck. A look of puzzlement on his face, he fell first to his knees and then to the floor. As his vision faded, he just had the time to see a man landing back on the ground some distance away, as if he had delivered the blow with his outstretched hand. His feet seeming to not even touch the ground, Sumara rushed forward to pull the sentry's body silently into the shadows. Dash watched from his hiding place, his antenna tail wagging furiously in delight.

From behind the wall, Jhy opened his eyes to break his psychic link with his dog. 'Now!' he beamed. He joined Lovell and Clarence to scramble over the rubble and through the gap in the wall made by the freighter. Approaching the forward hull of the broken ship, Lovell held up a hand. Leaning in close, he whispered into the debris.

'Rudy?' he rasped, urgently. There was a silence. Clarence and Lovell stole an anxious look. 'Rudy, are you there?'

'Yes, sir,' came a rasping voice at last. Clarence beamed in response and squeezed Jhy by the shoulder in celebration.

'Okay,' cautioned Lovell. 'Keep your voice down and get out as soon as possible.'

'Thank you, sir,' boomed Rudy, much too loud. 'Thank you, sir.'

Sensing a sudden movement above him, Lovell tensed. Looking slowly up, he saw a Zargon guard staring curiously down at him. Just as he reached up to tap at his comms unit, Clarence swung his long arms to sweep the guard's legs from beneath him. As he hit the ground, Lovell leaped forward to finish the job, smashing the butt of his rifle on the sentry's head. Panting, he looked around for signs of them having been discovered. Nothing. Lovell breathed a sigh of relief and motioned to his team to follow him. Moving close to the ground, the little party crept away from the hole in the wall toward a large storage tank. Every now and then, they would dart into the shadows to avoid a sentry party or small teams of maintenance operatives sent to sure up the wall.

'Right kid,' Lovell breathed as they pressed themselves against the storage tank, 'it's your show. Find the main generator.' He nodded to a door in the interior wall. From his memory of the fortress' schematics, it led deep down into the stronghold's bowels. Nodding, Jhy reached down to pick up Dash, making soothing noises to calm him in his excitement. Picking his moment carefully, the boy tucked his dog under his arm and made his way behind the tank towards the doorway. Ducking back into the shadows as a sentry patrol marched passed by, he cautioned his robot pet to be quiet. The guards out of sight and earshot, he sprang towards the door.

'Be careful, Dash,' Jhy whispered into his dog's ear. 'Go find it.'

As he opened the door, Dash bounded excitedly through to the tunnel beyond. As soon as he was out of sight, Jhy closed the door gingerly behind him and crept back to his companions at the storage tank. Lovell was looking with concern towards the wreckage of his ship. The rubble around it was starting to move. Rudy was pushing his way out.

'Quiet, Rudy,' Lovell whispered to himself, concerned at the noise. 'You clumsy great – '

'Why are you always picking on him?'

Lovell looked down to see Jhy gazing back with wide, accusing eyes. 'Him?' Lovell snapped. '*Him* is an *it*, and *it* is a *machine*. You concentrate on Dash.'

Gritting his teeth in frustration, Jhy squeezed his eyes shut.

Lovell's attention was drawn to a sudden movement by his freighter. A large boulder had been dislodged to reveal Rudy's huge head peering through. Shaking the dust from his shoulders, the enormous robot heaved himself from the wreckage. Looking anxiously to the wall beyond, Lovell could see a sentry on patrol right above him. Rudy froze, his enormous frame seeming to become just another piece of debris dislodged by the impact. Looking about him, the sentry moved off in the opposite direction to resume his patrol. Lovell waved for Rudy to make a run for it. Just as the robot lurched forward, however, Lovell could see the sentry returning. If he reached the edge of the wall in time, he was sure to see Rudy lumbering toward the storage tank. Lovell waved again, desperate to hurry Rudy along. At last, he joined him at the storage tank. Jhy flung himself around the great robot's legs while Clarence reached up to clap him heartily on the shoulder.

'Well done, Rudy,' the chimp enthused. 'Great flying.'

'The flying was easy, sir,' Rudy replied, his sensor eyes twinkling. 'Crashing was the difficult part.'

'Yeah, Rudy,' offered Lovell, reluctantly. 'Great job.'

Rudy gave a small bow in gratitude, then turned to Sumara. The mystic smiled back and nodded in admiration. 'Your self control in the face of danger was exemplary,' he beamed.

'That means the most of all,' Rudy boomed, as emotional as a robot could get.

'Hey!' Lovell hissed. 'Keep it down, will you? We're not there yet.' He turned to Jhy. 'Where's Dash?'

Obediently, Jhy snapped his eyes shut to make contact with his pet. The image quickly resolved itself in his mind's eye. Dash was moving through another of the seemingly endless corridors in the underground complex. A red cable hung from the wall. Finally, he came to a steel door. Dash stopped to survey the scene, his sensors picking out a control panel mounted on the wall. Activating his mini thrusters, the little robot lifted off the floor to punch at the buttons with his nose. Jhy saw the door slide open and felt Dash fly swiftly through. He was in an immense generator room, the main power source of the complex. From the robot's position on a metallic walkway, Jhy could see four huge metallic tubes filling the central area. Around the walls, a series of sophisticated control panels blinked on and off to the accompaniment of whirring fans.

'He's in,' Jhy explained, to the relief of the rest of his group. 'In the middle are these… *machines.*' He cocked his head as if listening. 'They're making a noise.'

'What noise?' Lovell was suddenly concerned.

'A sort of loud hum.'

Clarence nodded, knowingly. 'Nuclear turbines,' he said.

'There's something else.' Jhy was concentrating hard. 'He's getting a reading. Slight radiation.'

'That's it!' exclaimed Clarence, excitedly. 'That's where we plant the explosives.'

'Okay, kid. Get him outta there.'

Jhy squeezed his eyes tighter shut. 'Here, Dash!' he called, as loud as he dared.

As they waited for the dog to return, the little group prepared themselves for the final assault. Clarence and Lovell checked their guns, while Jhy and Sumara began priming the explosives from their packs.

Just as Jhy drew the string on his pack, he stood bolt upright, a look of alarm on his face. 'They've got him,' he breathed in terror.

Dash had been hurrying back through the maze of corridors, intent on obeying his master's command to return. He was already processing the visual data he had acquired in the generator room. Just as he had determined the exact level of radiation in the room and just how dangerous it would prove to his more vulnerable companions, he had been stopped dead in his tracks by the approach of several Zargon soldiers. He had turned swiftly to retrace his steps in hopes of discovering an escape route, only to be confronted by yet more soldiers. His only route of retreat had been cut off. Referring to the schematics he carried in his tiny robot brain, he had seen this corridor had no doorways, access panels or side passages down which to bolt. In response to the dire circumstances in which he had suddenly found himself, Dash had done the only thing he could do. He had cut off his mini-thrusters, closed down all his programs and fallen to the floor.

'Some kind of drone,' reported a lead soldier as he bent down to retrieve the unit.

'Let's take it to the labs,' hissed another over the open comms. 'See what makes him tick.'

'Who's got him?' Lovell demanded.

Jhy was close to tears. 'Soldiers,' he sobbed. 'I can feel it.' He looked desperately around him. Rudy hung his head in sadness, Clarence stared, unsure of what to say while Sumara stepped forward to lay a consoling hand on the boy's arm.

Jhy stared imploringly at Lovell, his eyes beginning to fill with tears. 'We have to do something. They'll kill him.'

Lovell dropped to his haunches and held the boy by the shoulders. 'I'm sorry, kid,' he said, meeting his gaze, 'but there's not a lot we can do about it.'

'But – '

As Jhy continued to protest, Lovell stood back up. 'Let's move,' he said, a note of determination in his voice. Sadly, the group made their final preparations to follow Dash through the door.

'Now we know we're gonna meet resistance,' warned Clarence as he handed out the laser guns. 'And if they've got Dash, they'll know we're coming.'

Just as the chimp handed a weapon to Sumara, Jhy rushed forward to grab the gun from his hands. 'Hey!' Clarence squealed in surprise. Jhy cocked the gun in response, expertly setting the controls.

Lovell was impressed. 'You sure you can handle that?'

Jhy held the gun before him, his young face now grimly determined. 'Watch me.'

Lovell nodded. He understood. This was no longer about the money. Now the guards had Dash, it was personal. Cocking his own gun and looking around him to ready his party, Lovell threw a look to Rudy.

'Do I have to try and be quiet?' the great robot grumbled, guiltily.

In seeming defiance of the desperate situation in which they found themselves, Lovell broke into a broad grin. 'Make as much damned noise as you like,' he beamed. 'Go!'

The effect of his command was startling. Almost as one, the little group tensed for action, then rushed forwards with a release of energy. The storage tank that had provided them with shelter from the guards was twenty yards from the doorway in the rock. They had traversed the distance in moments, their weapons bristling before them.

Rudy let out an ear-splitting yell as he lumbered towards the door, the ground beneath him seeming to shake with every heavy footstep. As they reached the door, they saw they were now in line of sight of the sentries on the wall. With shouts of alarm, the guards shouldered their HE Guns and opened fire. A hail of ice bullets fell like nails around Lovell and his raiding party. Sensing the danger, Rudy spread his arms. The bullets bounced harmlessly off his armour as he provided shelter for those behind him.

'Nice work!' called Clarence as he grappled with the door.

'I live to serve, sir,' replied Rudy, drolly.

Falling to his knees and taking shelter behind one of the huge robot's mighty legs, Jhy levelled his laser gun. 'This is for Dash,' he hissed as he squeezed the trigger.

Fizzing through the air at the speed of light, the laser bolt hit a sentry square in the chest. With a blood curdling scream that Jhy could hear from his position almost a quarter of a mile away, the sentry fell from his post, twisting through the air to land with a crunch on the freighter debris.

'Rudy, I need you!' Clarence called desperately from the door. Turning his monstrous head, Rudy could see that the chimpanzee had made no progress with the door. 'They must've engaged their security protocols,' Clarence called. 'The door's locked.'

Rudy nodded in understanding. 'You'll be losing your cover,' he growled to Lovell and the others, 'in three… two… one!'

With that, the party dropped to their knees, guns blazing as Rudy spun round to the door. The sentries on the wall fell back under the sudden blitz of fire, groping for shelter behind whatever rock or brickwork they could find. Several of them fell where they ran, caught in the back by a laser, their legs buckling beneath them, their arms flailing in agony.

Bunching his hands into formidable fists, Rudy pummelled at the door until the metal buckled out of shape. Grabbing the distorted panel with his fingers, he tore the door from its hinges as if it were cardboard. Throwing it to one side, he gave a look to Sumara. *This is no time for delicacy*, he seemed to say. Sumara smiled. Lovell looked behind him to see the way to the interior of the complex was now clear. 'We're in!' he shouted, and he led his group through the door.

XVII

PROGRESS

The laboratory was pristine. The light from a central ceiling lamp bounced off the gleaming white walls and metal instruments. Dash had been placed unceremoniously in the middle of a wide metal operating board.

'It's an automaton, sir,' the technician announced.

Grand Leutna Gahn nodded, leaning in for a closer look at the robot dog. 'Function?' he growled, flexing a new baton in his hands.

'We would need to remove the head, sir,' the technician blinked.

'Do it,' Gahn barked.

He watched as the technician crossed to a unit on the wall and retrieved a portable circular saw. At the flick of a switch, the vicious blades became a blur. The flicker of a smile crossed the Grand Leutna's face. He was looking forward to this. Just as the technician's blade grazed the robot dog's neck, a noise at the door interrupted the operation.

'Intruders in section four,' Braxx panted, standing to attention as he spoke.

Grand Leutna Gahn frowned at the interruption. 'Sound a general alarm,' he snapped. As the soldier turned back to the door, Gahn waved the technician away. 'This will have to wait,' he grumbled, his face clouded with anger. 'When the intruders are caught, I will personally supervise their annihilation.'

An urgent klaxon was sounding throughout the complex as the raiding party ran through the corridor. Lights flashed red on the walls, disorientating Lovell and his group as they pushed forward. As they turned a corner to the generator room, a steel door hissed shut before them, blocking their progress.

'Rudy!' Lovell called.

The giant robot tensed his upper body and barrelled towards the door. It bent with the impact. 'Again!' Lovell commanded and Rudy retreated a few steps to gather speed. Lowering his head to use as a battering ram, Rudy ran at the door again. This time it buckled and the robot smashed through. Using his immensely powerful arms, he wrenched back the jagged edges of the metal to form an opening.

'Good work!' called Lovell as he led the way through. Just as the group crossed the threshold, a burst of gunfire glanced off the walls around them. Turning, Lovell saw three Zargon guards crouching low back down the corridor. 'We got company!' Lovell yelled. Beyond the crouching soldiers, four more had appeared at the opening to the complex, two of them lifting the discarded door to use as a shield as they fired. Jhy and Clarence dropped to their knees to return fire. Pulling an explosive device from one of the backpacks, Lovell stood to take aim. Swinging his arm behind and over, he let go the device as it reached the apex of the arc. Flying gracefully through the corridor, it landed with a clatter at the feet of the first group of guards. There was a moment of confusion as the Zargons looked at each other, then the device detonated between them with a flash of intense light that sent them reeling.

Lovell urged Rudy before them as they moved on through the corridor to the generator room. More guards had appeared between them and their target. 'Rudy!' Lovell called through the cacophony, 'we need cover!' Rudy spread his arms wide and walked into the hail of gunfire from the guards that awaited them. The soldiers raked the corridor with a hale of fire as they squatted on the floor, but their ice bullets bounced harmlessly off Rudy's broad chest. Clarence levelled his weapon beneath Rudy's wide arms as they pushed forward. Laser bolts flashed down the corridor, slicing into the guards where they crouched, hopelessly outgunned. Bringing up the rear, Jhy and Lovell picked off the Zargons further back down the tunnel as they staggered to their feet following the explosive blast. At last they came to a T-junction. Corridors led away to the left and the right, both of them filling with yet more Zargon guards.

'Which way, kid?' shouted Lovell above the maelstrom. He leaned around Rudy's thick legs to let loose a volley of shots.

'I don't know!' replied Jhy, apologetically.

'Think!' Lovell insisted as another group of guards came to join their comrades. 'Which way did Dash go to the generator?'

Clarence was concentrating his fire forward now, leaning to the left and right to pick off the guards in each fork of the T-junction.

'Left!' squealed Jhy suddenly, pointing at a red cable slung from the corridor wall. 'He went left! I remember the cable!'

'Nice work, Jhy,' Lovell beamed, waving the group forward. 'Okay, Rudy, go left!'

Before them, a contingent of Zargons ran along the corridor towards the intersection to join the action. Lovell noticed them moving in a triangular formation with an officer at the head. 'Hang back, Rudy!' he commanded, lifting a flap on Jhy's pack. Checking that the guards had maintained their formation, Lovell hurled another explosive ball down the corridor towards them. Before they'd even had time to respond, the device exploded in front of the lead officer, sending him flying back into his soldiers.

'Strike!' called Lovell in triumph as he turned to Clarence.

The chimpanzee did not look impressed. 'Let's just keep our eye on the prize, shall we, Lovell?'

Lovell peered over Rudy's shoulder to see one soldier staggering to his feet. 'Dammit,' the captain seethed as he picked him off with his laser. 'Let's call it a spare.'

Pushing forward with all guns blazing, Lovell and his gang were soon standing outside a heavy steel door.

'That's it!' scream Jhy, excitedly. 'That's the generator room!'

The corridor had filled with smoke as they advanced and Lovell was firing blindly into the smog around them. Luckily, the Zargon forces were encountering a similar problem. Ice bullets embedded themselves in the walls and ceiling or bounced harmlessly off Rudy's inch thick plating.

'Smash the door, Rudy!' Lovell yelled as he fired.

Obediently, the robot pounded at the door. 'This one's thick, sir,' he complained.

'I've got every faith in you!' Lovell shouted in encouragement.

'Lovell!' Sumara was pointing ahead where, in the smoke, a light grenade was arcing through the air.

'Incoming!' yelled Lovell, sheltering as best he could behind Rudy's giant legs. The robot moved as swiftly as he could to a nearby alcove to provide some shelter. Clarence placed his hands over Jhy's eyes to save him from the worst effects of the blast. Sumara looked around to see his colleagues had taken cover as best they could, then closed his eyes. Lovell looked on in wonder as a look of calm fell over the mystic's face. He reached a hand out in front of him, as if he was to catch a ball. Glancing up the corridor, Lovell saw the light grenade stop in mid air. Sumara clenched his hand, then swung his arm forward to let it go. Several yards away, the light grenade swung through the air then hurtled back up the corridor towards the Zargon guards. Lovell allowed himself a wry smile. *Bet they weren't expecting that.* The grenade exploded with a *crump*, scattering the Zargon guards.

Glancing from the alcove, Lovell saw Rudy reaching across the corridor to batter the steel door to the generator room. The captain looked desperate. 'Hurry it up!' he yelled as the smoke began to clear. From the increase in gunfire, he knew more guards were approaching. Pretty soon, they'd be sitting ducks. He leaned out from the alcove to deliver another volley of laser fire up the corridor. Jhy and Clarence followed his lead and, once again, the criss-cross of laser bolts lit up the air. Rudy was trying again, throwing all his weight behind his fists to smash at the steel door. 'How the hell did Dash get in?' Lovell screamed to Jhy.

The boy ceased firing long enough to point up to a control panel on the wall. Lovell rolled his eyes. 'Well, why didn't you say so?' he sighed. 'Hey! Rudy! Down!'

Without questioning the command, Rudy dropped to one knee and bowed his head. Using the robot's body for protection against the gunfire, Lovell sprang across the corridor and onto Rudy's bent knee. In a single action, he punched at the control panel and rolled through the opening door, his companions following swiftly behind.

'Hold the door!' Lovell shouted after a swift headcount. With all the raiding party inside, he punched at a control panel on the wall. The heavy steel door hissed back into place. Rudy edged his huge bulk into the doorframe, leaning against the door to prevent it opening again.

'I've got it, sir,' he said. 'But I don't know how long it'll hold.'

Lovell and Clarence inched along the metal gantry stretching across the room, looking down to the huge nuclear turbines below. 'Remember,' Clarence was panting. 'The radiation in here will be dangerous to us given enough time. We gotta be in and out.'

'Got it,' Lovell replied, nodding over to where a covered ladder led down to the floor below. Swinging his leg over the top rung, he led the way down to the turbines. 'Jhy!' he called back. 'You and Sumara stay with Rudy. If that door fails, you're gonna have to keep the Zargons back.' Jhy nodded and ran to Sumara's side, his gun raised.

'The door's getting hot!' Rudy boomed.

'They must be using the heat exhausts on their HE Guns,' Sumara explained. 'But don't worry. As I often say, the only way to beat the heat is to *think* yourself cool.' As Jhy watched, the mystic's expression turned to one of absolute calm. He held his hands before him and Jhy could see beads of sweat starting to form on their backs. Soon, his face ran with perspiration, despite the fact that he was several metres from the door. 'Thanks!' called Rudy. 'That's much better!' Jhy nodded in awe. Sumara was draining some of the heat away from Rudy's circuits, seemingly obvious to the harm he might do himself.

Meanwhile, having climbed down to the lower level, Lovell and Clarence were searching around in the mass of pipes and cable ducts linking the huge turbines. At last, Clarence found what he was looking for.

'That's it!' he exclaimed. 'Main turbo inlet.' Gingerly, Clarence took a wrench-like tool from his bag and began to unscrew an inspection cover.

On the upper level, the guards had cut a slot into the door with their flame guns. Now, using a long crowbar as a lever through the hole to the floor, they were straining to prise the entrance open. Rudy was emitting strange, mechanical grunts in an effort to keep the door from sliding open. His massive hands bit into the metal in his endeavour to keep it closed.

'Got it.' Clarence carefully removed the inspection cover.

'You sure this will work?' Lovell was looking nervous beside him.

'If there's one thing I know about,' the chimp retorted unconvincingly, 'it's nuclear turbines.' As he reached into his tunic pocket, he became aware that the noise at the door had stopped.

'What's going on up there?' called Lovell, straining his neck to see.

The crowbar had been withdrawn. Rudy was listening hard. 'I can't believe they've given up,' he growled. He could hear scuffling noises from behind the door.

Below him, Clarence was inserting a small cylindrical container into the inspection panel.

'Is that it?' Lovell whispered.

Clarence grinned a toothy grin. 'That's it. When it reaches the energy exchanger, the whole plant will go critical.'

Lovell nodded. 'Boom?'

'Boom.'

'How long?'

Clarence looked suddenly serious. 'We have exactly thirty minutes. Not a minute more.'

'Okay.' Lovell called up the ladder to his companions. 'Stand by! We're getting outta here!'

'Er, Lovell?' Rudy called back, his visual sensors blinking with concern. 'We may have a problem.'

Lovell hauled himself from the top rung of the ladder back onto the gantry. 'What is it, Rudy?'

'I was right, they hadn't given up.' The robot was peering through the gap made in the door by the soldiers' HE Guns.

'What is it?' Clarence was panting as he joined them. 'What do you see?'

Rudy's huge head swivelled round to look directly at him. 'Grenades,' he said. Before anyone had even the smallest chance to react, there came a searing flash from the door and a blast wave propelled everyone back into the room. A ball of smoke and flame ripped through the air as the crack of an explosion shook the walls.

As the debris settled, Lovell lifted his head from the floor where he had landed. Almost comically, he saw that the entire wall around the door had been blown away, leaving Rudy standing, seemingly completely untouched, with the remnants of the door still clutched in his hands. Looking around in the confusion, Lovell saw that the blast had released another door in the room.

'Rudy! Everybody!' he yelled. 'Let's go!' Making use of the cover afforded them by the smoke, the raiding party made for the door and found themselves in an almost identical corridor. Slamming the door shut behind them, Rudy raised a huge fist and drove it into the control panel on the wall. It sparked and popped as the locks were engaged.

'That should hold them a while,' the robot boomed, pleased with himself.

The Grand Leutna was fuming. 'Five of them,' he hissed as he paced along the observation window in his quarters. 'And they outrun, outfight and out-think the entire resources of this base.' He turned to glare at Leutna Braxx who stood, shuffling uncomfortably from foot to foot. 'Who is this Lovell?'

Braxx swallowed. 'He's an Earthman, sir.'

Grand Leutna Gahn turned to stare out over the asteroid beyond the glass. 'An Earthman,' he mused. 'They have the weakness of sentimentality.'

The words hung in the air for a while as Braxx considered the implications. 'I think I know his weakness,' he said with a smile. Gahn turned, his eyebrows raised in expectation. Braxx reached for his comms unit. 'Have the Kestran Colonel brought to the Grand Leutna's private quarters,' he commanded.

Gahn nodded in understanding. The Intelligence Captain that he had placed in Zana's retinue had reported that she and Lovell shared something of a bond. It was time to test just how strong it was. 'Have the Captain meet Lovell to break the news.'

As Braxx saluted and left the room, the Grand Leutna turned back to the window. 'Visual!' he barked. 'Show me the countdown.' The screen blinked into life, the countdown clock ticking remorselessly down towards detonation.

'Countdown continues,' came a computer voice.

Gahn gnawed at his lip. 'Commence phase four,' he commanded.

Lovell waved his group on along the corridor. With the device planted in the turbine inspection hatch, the priority was to get out as soon as possible. As they rounded a corner, they were forced to take cover behind a bulkhead as two Zargon soldiers approached, their HE Guns blazing. It took a moment for Clarence and Lovell to pick them off and soon they were stepping around their bodies on their way to the exit.

'We're almost through,' Lovell grinned, ruffling Jhy's hair in celebration.

'Wait!' cautioned Clarence, suddenly. 'Listen.'

The little group fell silent, each of them tensed in expectation. And then they heard it. Footsteps were echoing down the corridor towards them. Not the rushing of soldiers, but a slow shambling gait.

'Get ready to fire,' Lovell whispered as he and Clarence lifted their weapons.

As they readied themselves for action, they saw a man turn the corner before them. He had the distinctive almond eyes of all his race and wore a Kestran captain's uniform. Lovell saw that his hair was dishevelled and the shoulder of his tunic was torn.

'Lovell,' the Captain rasped. 'Please, don't shoot.' He raised his hands above his head and shuffled feebly forwards.

'Who are you?' Lovell narrowed his eyes. He lowered his weapon, but kept his finger on the trigger.

'Captain Arric Thawn,' the man replied. 'Kestran Intelligence.'

Clarence had kept his gun up. 'What are you doing here?'

The Captain took a breath and looked around him. 'We were space-jacked,' he whispered.

Lovell cocked his head, suspicious. 'We?'

'They have Colonel Zana.'

Lovell was aghast. 'What? How?'

'He's lying,' Jhy snapped at once.

Captain Thawn took a step forward. 'No,' he protested. 'It's the truth.'

Lovell looked at the boy by his side. Jhy was staring intently at the Captain. 'Well,' he said, 'he's lying about something.'

Lovell leaned closer. 'What is it?' he asked from the corner of his mouth, keeping his eyes on the Captain before him. 'Read his mind, kid.'

Jhy moved his head from side to side in anguish. 'I can't,' he moaned. 'I switched off.'

'Switched off?' Clarence was leaning closer now, eager to hear.

Jhy nodded. 'My link with Dash. When they were killing him, I switched off my psychic eye.' Lovell noticed tears on his cheeks. 'If I open it again to read the Captain's mind, I'll see what happened to Dash.' He looked hopelessly to Lovell who nodded in understanding.

'We're here for you kid,' he murmured, 'but we've got to know what this man's hiding.'

Swallowing hard in resignation, Jhy squeezed his eyes tight shut. Lovell noticed the Captain backing slowly away. Lovell looked back to Jhy. 'What d'ya see, kid?' The boy beside him was murmuring feverishly as he re-established his psychic link.

'I see Dash,' he mumbled. 'On a table. Helpless.' Jhy grit his teeth.

'Focus on the Captain,' Sumara soothed from behind him. 'That will help.' He placed a hand on the boy's shoulder in sympathy.

Torn by indecision, Jhy grit is teeth. Suddenly, he gasped and ducked away from Sumara's hand.

'What did you see?' Lovell's eyes were wide with concern.

'A saw,' Jhy stuttered, his whole body trembling. 'A circular saw. Getting closer and closer. I can't bear it.'

'The Captain,' Sumara intoned. 'Focus on the Captain. Let me take your fear upon myself.' Lovell glanced behind him to see Sumara was closing his eyes too. In a moment, Jhy's anguished expression was replaced with one of utter calm. Lovell noticed Sumara wince as he took on Jhy's pain.

'There,' the mystic whispered. 'I have it. I feel it. Now, the Captain.'

Released from his agony, Jhy reached out towards Captain Thawn with his thoughts, probing the corners of his mind. Suddenly, his eyes snapped open. 'He's a traitor!' he yelled. With that, he fainted clean away. Lovell let his gun drop to the floor. He reached out instinctively to break Jhy's fall as Clarence leaned over to support him.

Taking advantage of the confusion, the Captain lunged towards the chimp and snatched his gun away. Rudy took the opportunity to step behind him, breaking any chance he had of escaping back down the corridor. 'Alright,' the Captain panted. 'Let the kid go.'

Glaring at the Captain in fury, Lovell lowered Jhy slowly to the floor.

'Now, everyone, back away.' Captain Thawn had Clarence's laser gun aimed before him. 'Nice and slowly.'

As Lovell, Clarence and Sumara stepped away from the boy, they each noticed Rudy pulling himself up to his full height behind the Captain.

'You lose, Lovell,' grinned Thawn, levelling his gun again. 'Sorry to break up the party.' Just as he squeezed the trigger to shoot, Lovell saw Rudy raise a huge fist behind the Captain. Preparing to bring it down with a crushing blow on the man's head, the giant robot suddenly froze in position. Lovell's eyes flicked to the gun in the Captain's hand. It seemed to take an age for him to release the laser bolt from the muzzle. In the meantime, Rudy was standing stock still behind him, his arm raised in preparation for the killer blow. But it never came. Noticing Lovell's look, the Captain turned slightly to look over his shoulder, suddenly concerned that he might be in danger. That was all the distraction Sumara needed.

Seizing his chance, the mystic leaped forward, swinging his leg in the air before him. The Captain reacted as if he'd taken a blow to the chin. With a grunt of surprise, he sunk to the floor, the gun clattering from his hand. Lovell lurched forward to retrieve his weapon and trained it on the Captain where he lay, dazed and flailing on the ground. 'The party's not over yet,' he grinned.

'Why, Rudy?' Clarence was approaching the giant robot with caution. Rudy's arms hung by his side once more and his head was lowered. He looked as despondent as any robot could. 'What happened?'

'Safety protocols,' he said, sadly. 'I cannot directly harm any humanoid life form.'

'Concern for the sanctity of life is admirable,' Sumara said, patting Rudy on his shoulder plating. 'You should not feel sorry for it.'

Just as Lovell was about to respond, he saw Jhy moving on the floor. Bending down to the boy, he helped him sit up, then supported him as he rose shakily to his feet.

'Well done, kid,' Lovell said softly. 'You did well.'

Jhy saw the Captain lying on the floor and nodded. Then, he turned with urgency to Lovell. 'Dash is alive,' he said, hurriedly. 'They're holding him, and Colonel Zana, too'.

Clarence turned to the boy and cocked his laser gun. 'Then let's go get them.'

XVIII

THE RESCUE

The stairway outside the Grand Leutna's private quarters was heavily guarded.

'That's it,' said Jhy, pointing to the glass doors at the top of the stairs. 'That's where they're keeping Colonel Zana.'

As the group took shelter behind a metal rampart, Lovell puffed out his cheeks. 'Looks like they're waiting for us.' Looking around the open area at the foot of the stairs, he could see groups of soldiers standing guard, their guns at the ready. Some had positioned themselves behind swiftly erected barricades of metal plate.

'So how do we get in there?' Clarence jabbed a hairy finger towards the Grand Leutna's quarters.

Lovell turned to Rudy who was skulking in the shadows behind them. 'You're the only one who's got a chance of making it.'

Rudy shrugged, still downcast. 'I cannot fight, sir.'

'Dash and Zana are up there,' Lovell pleaded. 'You can save them.'

Rudy shook his great head in response. 'I'm sorry,' he mumbled.

'I will go.' Sumara had stepped forward from the shadows.

Lovell swivelled round to face him. 'It's too dangerous for anyone but Rudy,' he said. 'Look around you.' He gestured to the groups of soldiers scattered before them. 'You'd be taking your life in your own hands.'

Sumara smiled, patiently. 'You forget, John Lovell. Death is of no consequence to me.'

Meeting his gaze, Lovell could see he was adamant. He turned to his companions. 'Cover him.'

The group took a collective breath, preparing for battle. Lovell made eye contact with each one of them in turn. 'Whatever happens,' he said softly, 'I'm proud of what we've done. A good friend once told me that, sometimes, doing the right thing is the right thing to do.' He caught Clarence's eye as he spoke. 'That's never been truer than today.' He cocked his gun in readiness. 'Let's do the right thing.'

Rudy flung himself forwards at once. Although he could not knowingly harm a living soul, he could certainly draw their fire. Almost instantly, the guards trained their HE Guns upon him. Ice bullets flew through the air as Lovell, Jhy and Clarence all knelt to take aim. The air was lit with the flaming exhausts of the guard's guns and the criss cross of lasers. Lovell threw an explosive device into a group of guards by the stairs, sending them scattering in all directions to find cover. Zargon Light Grenades flashed violently in the ensuing chaos and the air filled with an acrid smoke. In the midst of it all, Sumara stood for a moment in deep meditation, his hands pressed palm to palm. Then, with an ear-splitting yell of defiance, he leaped from behind the rampart. Choosing his moment with care, he vaulted one of the makeshift barricades and disposed of two Zargon soldiers with a chop to their necks. Ducking down behind the metal plates, he sheltered from the blizzard of ice bullets and lasers fizzing around him.

Just as Lovell was about to make use of the diversion and press forward, he saw a Light Grenade arcing through the air towards him. It clattered to the floor several feet away; too far to reach, but close enough to do some serious damage. Turning, Rudy sensed the danger and reacted the only way he knew how. Throwing himself over the grenade as it exploded, he used the weight of his metal body to absorb the impact. Lovell saw the giant lift of the ground just a fraction of an inch as the grenade flashed viciously beneath him. Suddenly, a sharp pain stabbed at his shoulder. Lovell looked down. An ice bullet had grazed his arm, embedding itself harmlessly in the wall behind him. But it was an indication of just how much danger they were all in. He levelled his gun in response, unleashing a blast of laser fire that raked through a group of soldiers at the base of the stairs. They fell where they stood, clutching at their limbs and bodies in pain.

The soldiers incapacitated, Sumara wove and ducked his way to the stairway up to the Grand Leutna's quarters.

'Cover him!' Lovell screamed above the din, and the little raiding party concentrated their fire on the remaining soldiers. One of the soldiers, however, escaped their attention. Lifting his HE Gun to aim at Sumara as he bolted up the stairs, the Zargon squeezed his trigger. There was a burst of flame from his gun's exhaust and a hail of ice bullets rained down upon the staircase. Sumara didn't stand a chance. The impact sent him spinning back down to the floor, his body twisting under the impact of bullet after bullet.

Seeing his mentor hit the ground, Rudy made an almighty roar and leaped to his defence. The ground shook as he landed over his friend's crumpled body, shielding the mystic from the worst of the soldiers' gunfire. In relative safety, Sumara had a chance to heal. Bending his head to watch, Rudy's visual sensors glowed in surprise. Where Sumara had been bloodied and scarred, his skin had begun to smooth over. In just a few moments, his torn robe was the only evidence of any injury. 'Thanks, old friend,' Sumara breathed, patting Rudy's giant leg.

With that, he gathered his strength and set off at superhuman speed up the staircase. Reaching the very top step, he twisted in the air to kick at the control panel on the wall. As the door slid open, he found himself standing in a short corridor leading to the Grand Leutna's personal rooms. And there, some twenty feet away, stood Leutna Braxx.

Having watched Sumara's progress through the glass, he was standing ready. Sumara saw he had a Light Grenade primed and ready to throw. A smile spreading slowly over his face, Braxx swung his arm back to throw the grenade. And found he couldn't let go. As the sounds of battle raged through the glass door, Sumara stood with his eyes tight shut. He looked the very epitome of calm. His arm was held out before him, his hand clasped around an invisible object. Braxx swung his arm again, trying desperately to let the grenade go. But his hand wouldn't open. A look of panic flashed across his face. Using his other hand, he tried in vain to prise his fingers open. The grenade was stuck fast. He flashed a look to Sumara, pleading for mercy. But it was too late. The grenade exploded in a ball of fire and Leutna Braxx fell to the floor, a blackened pile of clothing and limbs.

Released from his psychic efforts, Sumara suddenly felt the effects of his exertions. His strength waning, he leaned against the wall to catch his breath. Summoning all that remained of his powers, the mystic shuffled past Braxx's body to the entrance to Gahn's rooms. The doors sprung open unbidden and Sumara looked up to see the Grand Leutna himself in the centre of the room.

'I do so hate unexpected company,' Gahn leered. 'Why couldn't you make an appointment like everyone else?' Sumara blinked to clear his head. As his eyes focussed on the scene before him, he saw that Gahn had Colonel Zahn in a vice like grip. He was holding her as a shield.

'Let the woman go,' Sumara hissed. 'As you can see, I am injured and unarmed.' He swayed as he spoke, wincing in pain. 'It's me you want. Let her go.'

There was a pause as the Grand Leutna considered his options. He looked Sumara up and down then laughed. Barely five and a half feet tall and draped in a dishevelled robe, the man looked to be no threat at all. Holding his hands up with a grin, he let Colonel Zana go. She spun away from him and cowered by the wall.

'Leave us, Colonel Zana,' Sumara panted, gesturing to Gahn. 'We have business to attend to.'

Looking round to get her bearings, Zana noticed a small metal box lying on a table. She had a sudden memory of Lovell handing her his crew manifest back on Kestra. She recognised the unit as Jhy's robot dog. Feigning a trip on the floor, she reached out to switch the robot on as she passed and noticed its whiskers quivering in response.

'Get out,' the Grand Leutna rasped. Stumbling through the door, Zana saw Gahn reaching for something on his belt.

The two men squared up to each other. As Gahn raised a gloved hand, Sumara could see he had detached a baton from a loop on his belt. Pressing a switch in the handle, the Grand Leutna gave the mystic a sickening grin. An evil looking length of glowing energy extended from the baton's tip. Sumara gasped. He had heard of the Laser Whip but had never thought he might have to defend himself against one. He knew it for a formidable weapon. As soon as Colonel Zana disappeared from the room, Gahn shifted his weight forward and slashed the whip. With lightning speed, Sumara ducked away in time to see it strike the wall nearby. It left a deep burning slash in the metallic surface.

Recovering his balance and summoning his psychic strength, Sumara reached forward to grab at the flailing whip with his telekinetic powers. He yelped as his hands sustained ferocious burns, despite being feet away from the fearsome weapon. He felt his wounds taking their toll and, once more, his strength fading. Sumara leaned back against a pillar for support, his chest heaving with every breath.

Sensing his evident weakness, the Grand Leutna began to toy with his quarry. Slashing viciously at Sumara's arms and legs, Gahn let go a hideous laugh. It was time to finish this puny man. Taking careful aim, he slashed his whip at the cowering form before him. Its coils twisted and wound their way around Sumara's neck, burning into the flesh. The mystic tried desperately to pull the energy coil away but it was already deeply embedded. He could smell the stench of scorching flesh in his nostrils. Calling on his last reserves, Sumara reached out his torn hands to form a stranglehold in the air. Gahn's leering face suddenly fell to an expression of alarm. Dropping the whip, he clutched at his neck trying desperately to prise himself free from the invisible hands at his throat. Relentlessly, Sumara forced him down to his knees. Gasping for breath, the Grand Leutna reached forward in desperation, his eyes bulging in their sockets. His breathing came in fits and starts as he collapsed to the floor, the blood vessels in his face swelling a lustrous purple. Soon, he was still, his eyes staring sightlessly up at Sumara in dreadful accusation. The trace of an enigmatic smile forming on his lips, the mystic swayed on his feet for a moment. Then, his energy spent and all his powers used, he too collapsed to the floor.

'Sumara is dead.'

'What?' Lovell spun round to face Jhy. 'How do you know that?'

The boy raised his arm to point up the stairs to the doorway. 'Dash is through there. He just watched Sumara die.' Jhy's bottom lip quivered as he spoke.

From his position near the stairs, Rudy let out a low moan of anguish. Lovell noticed more soldiers appearing from adjacent corridors. One squad was fixing mobile laser cannons into position, clambering onto the seats behind to focus the double barrels.

'Oh boy,' breathed Lovell. 'Now we're in trouble. Nothing gets past them.'

'Oh, yeah?' snorted Clarence from his side. 'Looks like someone forgot to tell Rudy.'

Peering through the smoke, Lovell could see Rudy lumbering forward, seemingly unaffected by the concentrated fire the Zargon laser cannons threw at him. Batting away the laser bolts as if they were troublesome flies, Rudy climbed the stairway, moaning softly all the way.

Finally, he found himself in Gahn's quarters, standing over Sumara's body where he had fallen. Reaching down with his huge hands, he summoned all his powers of self-control to delicately uncoil the vicious strands of the Laser Whip from the mystic's neck. Rocking back on his haunches, he gently cradled Sumara's head in his arms. From somewhere deep inside the robot's massive chest, low rumbles of grief seemed to travel across the floor in waves.

Back outside the Grand Leutna's quarters, the soldiers were making their way up the stairs in pursuit of the marauding robot. Deactivating their Laser Cannons behind them, they fired off random volleys through the smoke as they made their way up the staircase. In the confusion, Lovell noticed a slight figure edging around the corners of the concourse. He squeezed his trigger in readiness, but there was something in the figure's movements that told him it would be no threat. Emerging from the shadows at last, Colonel Zana stepped forward, a weary smile on her face. Lovell smiled back and squeezed her shoulder. She looked tired but not broken.

'You okay?' he whispered.

Zana even managed a laugh. 'I've been better,' she said, her almond eyes squinting in the smoke.

Lovell nodded then turned to a delighted looking Clarence. 'How long?' he barked.

'Ten minutes, maybe,' the chimpanzee shrugged. 'And it's delightful to see you again, Colonel Zana. Come here often?' He threw a wink to the Colonel and Zana laughed again.

'Okay.' Lovell looked serious. 'Time to leave.'

'We can't,' said Zana suddenly, a look of horror on her face.

Lovell took her gently by the arm. 'In ten minutes, this place gets blown apart,' he explained, patiently.

'We've got to get to the passengers.' Zana snapped her arm away from Lovell's grip.

'What passengers?'

'From the space-jacked liner.'

Lovell sighed and scratched at his chin. 'Yeah,' he breathed. 'Your Intelligence Captain told us.'

'Turns out he was the Zargons' Intelligence Captain,' replied Zana, a note of sadness in her voice. 'We can't leave them here to be blown to pieces with the fortress.'

'Of course not.' Lovell tried to hide his reluctance. 'Do you know where they're being held?'

Rudy sat stock still on the floor, the body of his mentor cradled in his arms. He was aware of the approaching soldiers, but chose not to show it. They were about as much of a threat to him as a Gypso Fly to a Rhinoderm. The soldiers surrounded him, their weapons raised. At a command from their leader, they opened fire. Their ice bullets ricocheted off Rudy's armour plating, bouncing dangerously around the room. Two of the soldiers received damage to their legs as a result. They limped from the room with their hands clamped over their wounds. The soldiers that remained suddenly didn't look so confident. Peering carefully at the giant robot, the Patrol Leader could see they hadn't even left a scratch. With a gesture to his comrades, he motioned that they should turn their guns round to engage their flamethrowers. At another command, sheets of fire enveloped the robot, lighting the room with their grisly glow. Still, they had no effect. The soldiers looked to their superior for options. It was clear he had none left. Looking around, the Patrol Leader saw the Grand Leutna's body lying crumpled by the observation window. He punched at a comms unit on the desk. 'We need medics at the Grand Leutna's quarters. Now!'

'Er, sir?' came a voice in his helmet. 'I think we may have a problem.'

The Patrol Leader turned to see that Rudy was rising from the floor.

'I thought I could not kill,' his great voice rumbled, ominously. 'But I know now, that it is a simple question of imposing the will on the power of your actions.' He paused for a moment, looking down at the small figure of a man in the robes. 'A great man taught me I could be whatever I needed to be.' Suddenly aware that the huge robot stood between them and the door, the soldiers started backing away to whatever shelter they could find. 'Whatever I am, Sumara,' Rudy concluded, 'I owe it to you.' With that, he swivelled his huge head around the room, his visual sensors locating each of the soldiers where they cowered in fear. Two of them, he noticed, were already within reach.

With a grinding of gears, Rudy seemed to puff out his metal chest. With a turn of speed that belied his great bulk, he swung his arms about him, knocking the two soldiers through the opposite wall. Ice bullets raked through the air as the remaining soldiers panicked. Despite their leader trying to impose some pattern to their efforts, they fired randomly, more in desperation than in control.

'There's no way we can get to the other passengers,' said Lovell as more Zargon troops spilled onto the concourse from the surrounding corridors. 'We'll be cut to pieces.'

'I will not leave them,' Zana said with force. 'If I have to walk right through those soldiers to get to them, I will.'

'It's okay, Colonel Zana,' said Clarence, suddenly. 'I don't think that will be necessary.' Dropping his gun to his side, the chimp pointed to the top of the stairs. Almost on cue, a Zargon soldier came smashing through the glass doors to tumble down the steps.

'Rudy!' screamed Jhy in delight.

The giant pacifist robot was now a terrifying fighting machine. As the newly arrived soldiers levelled their weapons, Rudy bounded to the concourse, throwing bodies behind him as if they were nothing more than toys. Ice bullets bounced harmlessly off his broad back. With their options limited in the face of such an unstoppable force, the Zargons had obviously decided to throw everything they had at him. The Laser Cannons were reactivated, but even they barely left a scratch. With a mighty roar, Rudy brought his great arms smashing down upon a group of soldiers at their barricade. Lovell noticed a fierce red light glowed from the robot's visual sensors. 'The worm has turned,' he said grimly.

Stepping on bodies and discarded weapons, Rudy made his way to the little group, crushing everything and everyone in his path.

'Think you can hold them?' Lovell yelled above the din.

The great machine nodded, slyly. 'Leave it to me.'

With that, he spun back into the concourse, his arms whirling around him.

Making use of the diversion, Lovell readied his group to move off. 'How long?' he asked Clarence, already dreading the response.

Clarence lifted his watch and tapped at the dial. 'Minutes,' he warned, grimly.

Sure, they had kept to the shadows and most of the soldiers they encountered were more concerned with the developments at the Grand Leutna's quarters, but still Lovell was nervous. With time so short, they were clearly risking their own lives in order to rescue the Space Liner's passengers. What was that saying about being a dead hero?

'Here,' panted Zana at last. 'This is the door.'

Clarence reached inside his pack to retrieve a small magnetic detonation device. Just as he fixed it to the heavy steel door before him, a tremor shook the fortress.

'What was that?' asked Jhy, nervously.

'The explosive I planted in the turbine,' Clarence replied. 'This is just the beginning.' Lifting a flap on the magnetic device on the door, he pressed a button to prime it, then gestured that the group should back carefully away to a safe distance. 'Pretty soon it'll cascade through the fortress' systems.' He glanced at Lovell. 'We'll need to be gone by then.'

There was a jolt as the door cracked cleanly in half. Clarence had set the device to discharge its energy into the door itself. Much safer for the dozen or so passengers that he could now see cowering against the furthest wall in the little cell. As the door fell away, Zana stepped through to address the prisoners.

'Come with us!' she yelled. 'This whole place is going to blow, but we can get you all outta here.' She thought suddenly and turned to Lovell. 'Can't we?'

XIX

CASUALTIES OF WAR

Completely unaware of the fate of their leader in his private quarters, the six Battle Cruisers hove into orbit around the planet Kestra. The great tubular missile launchers that hung in their central cavities were primed. They throbbed with latent power. An audible countdown sounded throughout the hangars and corridors as technicians and soldiers ran to their duty stations in readiness. There were just minutes to go, and then Kestra would be dust.

Whilst one mighty war machine readied itself for a show of power, another was in trouble. At last the soldiers' firepower was having an effect, and Rudy was struggling. As the great robot fought to hold his ground, the soldiers poured their fire into him. Laser Cannons scorched him at point blank range. Ice bullets chipped away at his armour. Light Grenades burnt his digital retinas. Finally overcome, Rudy staggered and fell to his knees with a crash. He lifted his hands to his head in a vain attempt to protect his vital systems, but he knew it was too late. Even his virtually indestructible body couldn't take this kind of firepower. Summoning the last of his energy, he tried to rise again. The soldiers could almost smell his weakness. Pressing forward, they piled everything they had upon him. Lasers were pumped into him from all sides as they pressed home their sudden advantage. Raked by the relentless fire, Rudy twisted almost balletically where he stood. Caught for a moment in stillness, he seemed perfectly balanced on the balls of his metal feet. And then, like a great tree, he fell. The blazing fire continued as he met the ground with a crash. There was no coming back from this one. Finally, he lay spread-eagled on the ground, taking up most of the concourse with his mighty bulk. His metal fingers scrambled for purchase on the ground. And then all movement ceased. The firing stopped. Slowly at first, but then gaining in confidence, the soldiers moved closer to inspect their prey.

'He's finished,' rasped the patrol leader over his comms. He knelt down to watch as the light in Rudy's visual sensors dimmed and then died. 'We got him.' But his triumph was short lived. As he rose to his feet to address his troops, a low rumbling sound came from deep within the complex. The soldiers looked at each other, unsure what was happening or how to react. A sudden jolt almost knocked them from their feet and a section of the ceiling gave way above them. It smashed to the floor, releasing clouds of choking dust into the air. Now the whole floor seemed to be shaking. The Patrol Leader looked around in confusion.

'Now what?'

'This way!' screamed Lovell. The dazed passengers were following him down the corridor to the concourse. They screamed as the ground shook beneath their feet. A dislodged girder smashed to the floor, narrowly missing a father and his small child. The small party shared worried looks between them as they made their slow progress along the corridor.

'We're almost there!' Clarence called from his position at the rear. He tried to keep the note of panic from his voice. The ominous rumble was becoming a deafening roar. 'It's going critical,' he muttered fearfully to himself.

At last they reached the concourse. It was empty of soldiers now. Lovell guessed they were headed to the launch bays, making their preparations to flee the stricken asteroid. As the passengers fanned out, looking for an escape route, Lovell couldn't help but notice the large mass of twisted ironwork lying prostrate on the floor.

'Rudy!' screamed Jhy as he ran forward.

'Come on, kid,' Lovell yelled above the noise. 'We gotta keep moving.'

'We can't leave him,' the boy pleaded, holding Rudy's huge head in his hands.

'He's finished, Jhy. Dead.' Lovell reached down to catch the boy by the arm.

'How do you know?' Jhy looked angry. 'What do you know about robots? What do you know about *anything*?'

Lovell had no answer.

'We take him with us.' Jhy's face was set into a look of gritty determination.

'Hey!' called Clarence to some passengers. 'Give a chimp a hand here!'

Jhy watched as between them, Clarence and a handful of passengers pulled some dead Zargon soldiers from a Laser Cannon. Uncoupling the fearsome weapon, the chimpanzee released the cannon from its fixings and slid it from its platform.

'Let's get the robot on here!' Clarence called, clutching at a supporting pillar as the ground shook around him.

'Clarence!' yelled Lovell. 'We don't have time!'

'This is the day we do the right thing, Lovell,' Clarence snapped back. 'And we do the right thing by *everybody*.'

With their leader dead, all discipline among the Zargon soldiers had disappeared. Now, it was very much every man for himself. As they ran to the vast hangar in search of transport off the crumbling fortress, they didn't even stop to confront the little gang responsible for it. Clarence, Lovell and Jhy passed unremarked as they hauled Rudy into the launch bay, the passengers straggling behind them.

'What's the plan, Lovell?' Colonel Zana asked, her almond eyes wide.

Lovell nodded into the huge space before them. '*That's* the plan.'

Zana followed his gaze to see countless Space Fighters and Transport Ships lifting into the air. The great hangar door was lowering slowly before them, a huge ledge of rock descending to the horizontal. There, in a corner by a fuelling station, Zana saw the Space Liner.

'Let's go!' Lovell urged his party on. 'We've got just seconds!'

The rock was vibrating alarmingly around them. Columns of debris fell from the vaulted ceiling. Great girders and metal struts smashed to the floor. As they ran for the boarding ramp, Lovell saw a whole row of Space Fighters taken out by falling masonry. Everywhere, people were running for their lives. As the majority of the passengers began to pile on board the liner, some hung back to help Clarence and Jhy haul Rudy into the hold on his improvised gurney.

Lovell heard Zana take a breath beside him. 'The entrance!' she gasped. She was staring straight ahead at the opening to the launch bay. The huge rock door was closing with a blaring of klaxons.

'Emergency security protocols must have kicked in,' Clarence panted. 'They're designed to shut the fortress down in case of an imminent threat. They never thought the threat would come from the *inside*.'

'Where's the control?' Zana asked in alarm.

Clarence shrugged in response. 'I don't know.'

As the hinged platform continued its relentless progress, Lovell turned to the remainder of the passengers on the boarding ramp. 'Get aboard,' he rasped. 'Start the engines.'

'Wait,' Zana began as Lovell moved off. 'Where are you going?'

The captain nodded towards a Laser Cannon. 'Target practice,' he grinned.

With a final look, the Colonel followed Clarence, Jhy and the rest of the passengers onto the Space Liner. As he reached the top of the ramp, Jhy turned at a familiar humming sound.

A small, dog-shaped robot was skimming its way through the falling debris, its whiskers twitching excitedly.

'Dash!' the boy cried, tears springing to his eyes. 'Here, boy!' Clutching his pet in his arms, Jhy turned to join his companions in the Space Liner. Within moments, the engines were sparking into life.

Lovell ran towards the Laser Cannon, struggling to stay upright in face of the quakes shaking the fortress. The whole of the giant hangar shuddered as great chunks of rock crashed down from the roof. Clambering onto the platform, he took the seat behind the twin barrels and leaned forward over the controls. Glancing at the Liner's cockpit window, he saw the pilot had taken his place at the controls. Colonel Zana peered anxiously from the window.

Forcing himself to concentrate among the melee, Lovell trained his guns on the hangar door. His vision hampered by the surrounding smoke, he aimed the barrels in the general direction of the entrance and squeezed the controls. The lasers streaked through the hangar to land on their target. Lovell could see Zana waving desperately from the cockpit. He looked around him. The hangar was moments from collapse, but he had to get that door open. He grit his teeth and fired again. Another volley of laser fire hit its mark. The door broke free of its mechanism and hung at an angle in its aperture. 'Not enough,' Lovell growled to himself. He could hear the Liner's engines whining. It lifted from the ground a couple of inches as the pilot readied to make a quick escape. A whole section of the hangar wall collapsed behind it, exposing the interior of the asteroid. Lovell knew he had to blast a hole in that door but, having done that, would he have time to make it to the Space Liner?

'What the hell,' he said to himself with a smile. 'You never know until you try.' With that, he leaned on the cannon's controls. Laser fire raked the hangar door once more. This time it was enough to dislodge it completely. The giant entrance broke from its mountings, crashing out to fall the two thousand feet to the rocks below.

With a cry of triumph, Lovell punched the air and jumped from his seat. Leaping from the trolley he gestured through the cockpit window that Zana should begin retracting the boarding ramp. Lovell saw her punch at a control and turn to the pilot. The hangar falling down around his ears, the captain jumped on the ramp just as it disappeared and hurled himself through the airlock door. Immediately, there was a roar of engines and the Liner lifted clear off the ground. Dodging falling rock as it gathered speed through the hangar, it swung round to the entrance and surged out into the night.

As the Space Liner cleared the fortress, the hangar behind it was engulfed in a ball of flame. Lovell staggered to the cockpit as it climbed into space. Looking back on the asteroid, he watched open mouthed as a series of explosions ripped through the Zargon stronghold. The walled fortress crumbled and shattered as it blew apart. Fuel dumps ignited, launch pads erupted. The collapse of the hangar left a giant wedge missing from the rocky buttress, like a deep axe-cut in a tree. Finally, the whole of the tower toppled. A million tons of rock and steel crashed a thousand feet in a roaring, cascading, final demolition. The entire complex was reduced to dust.

'Look!' Zana exclaimed. Ahead of them, hanging in orbit around the planet Kestra, the six fearsome Battle Cruisers were erupting into balls of flame. 'Enlarge that image,' the Colonel breathed in excitement. The pilot toggled a control at her command, and the forward windshield was filled with the image of exploding ships. Zana gasped as she saw the huge Interplanetary Ballistic Missile Launchers spinning away harmlessly into space.

'The damage has reached their remote systems,' Clarence explained with a smile. 'Everything linked to the Zargon fortress, even by an innocent communication wave, has been destroyed.'

Kestra was safe.

XX

EULOGY

Rudy lay on the table, his systems wired up to an array of monitors and circuitry. Aside from the equipment, the room was clinical and empty of furniture. A harsh light bounced off the sterile, white walls. Beside the table, two technicians were bent over a readout. Nodding to his companion, one turned with a sigh to face the two mourners. Lovell stood with his arm draped around Jhy's shoulder.

'He's dead?' the boy ventured, softly.

The technician nodded.

Lovell squeezed Jhy by the shoulder. 'I'm sorry kid,' he whispered.

Jhy was close to tears. 'We'll bury him.'

Lovell shook his head, not entirely sure he'd heard correctly. 'Say, what?'

Jhy met his gaze, immovable.

'Look,' Lovell began. 'You don't bury machines.'

'We'll bury him,' Jhy interrupted. 'And we'll bury him properly.'

The small party stood by the light of Kestra's five moons. They were gathered on a small, flat area of ground among high sculptured rocks. The pillars of rock around them seemed to glow in the sunlight, giving a faintly religious feel to proceedings.

John D. Lovell felt distinctly uncomfortable. As stood with Clarence, Jhy and Zana, he couldn't help but see the ridiculousness of the situation. Before them, next to a freshly dug grave, lay a pile of soil. Rudy's bulk had been such that there had been some earth left over when they had filled in the hole.

'You ought to say something,' said Jhy as Lovell prepared to turn away. The captain sighed inwardly. They had just spent the best part of two hours burying a heap of steel and circuitry. What was he to say? All he knew was, he would have to tread carefully. The last thing he wanted was to upset the kid further.

'Dearly beloved,' he began, 'we are gathered here today - '

Warning looks from Zana and Clarence served to stop him in his tracks. Clearing his throat, Lovell tried again. He took a breath and tried to take stock of all that had happened.

'Rudy was a robot,' he said simply. 'A machine without feelings.' Seeing Clarence about to interrupt, he held up a hand to calm him and ploughed on. 'But when he saw a friend dead at his feet he became…' he searched for the words. 'He felt emotion. He felt anger and sorrow. And maybe that gave him a *kind* of life.' Lovell eyed Jhy carefully as he spoke. 'A true existence. And Rudy sacrificed this new found life to save his new found friends.' He looked around at the assembled group. 'That's all I can say,' he concluded.

The eulogy over, they turned away from the graveside and back towards the bustling streets of Estoran. Colonel Zana caught up with Lovell as they walked, linking her arm through his.

'Nice words,' she smiled. 'They really helped.' She cast a look behind them as she spoke, and saw Jhy hovering by the graveside.

'Kid needs some time alone,' nodded Lovell. 'To say goodbye to a heap of nuts and bolts.'

'Lovell!' Zana poked Lovell's arm. 'Just when I think I'm getting to like you.'

Just as they reached the ring of rocks that surrounded the small plain, they heard a shout.

'Hey!'

'What's up with Jhy?' Clarence was squinting through the sun.

Lovell and Zana turned to see the boy beckoning them back with some urgency. Rolling his eyes, Lovell trudged back through the dust as Zana moved on ahead. He saw her exchanging words with an excitable Jhy, then she walked back, quicker this time, to Lovell.

'There's something moving under the rocks,' she said, breathlessly.

Lovell raised his eyebrows. '*Something?*'

He was at the graveside now and peered down to the pile of rocks that stood as a memorial to the robot beneath.

'Look!' Jhy pointed at the base of the rocks. The earth was definitely shifting. Cracks were appearing in the dried mud. The dust was disappearing with increasing speed through the fissures, like sand in an hourglass. Suddenly, a giant fist pushed its way out to the surface.

There were gasps all round. 'Rudy?' Clarence had fallen to his knees to dig at the earth, showing no concern for the effect it had on his white tunic. Jhy leaped forward to throw rocks aside in an effort to help, Dash jumping excitedly at his side. But Rudy needed no assistance.

'He's alive!' Zana exclaimed, turning to a bemused Lovell.

The earth was crumbling as a central mound began to protrude from the grave. As if fell to the ground in clouds of dust, Lovell could make out the glint of metal in the sun. Finally, there was Rudy, standing tall. Even in the grave, he still towered over the assembled party. His great head turned to each of them in turn. Colonel Zana was beaming with excitement. Clarence seemed dumbstruck with awe, while Jhy could do nothing to hide his excitement.

'What happened?' the great robot asked, bemused.

Lovell shook his head. 'I can't begin to tell you.'

Rudy's visual sensors blinked, as if he was thinking things through. 'Did we... make it?' He stepped up from the grave and shook the dust from his great shoulders.

'Yes, Rudy!' Jhy jumped for joy and threw himself at the robot's leg.

Rudy nodded and turned his mechanical gaze on Lovell. 'Then, I can buy my freedom.'

Lovell shrugged. 'I guess.'

'What will you do with it?' Clarence was helping brush earth from his metal plating.

Rudy looked to Lovell again. 'Serve my master forever, of course.' He bowed his head reverently.

'Great,' Lovell sighed. 'That's all I need.' He took a moment to look at his companions. For the first time, he saw them as more than a team. They were his friends. 'Well,' he said, trying to ignore the rush of sentimentality, 'let's get out of here.'

Clarence ambled to his side, his knuckles dragging along the ground as he walked. 'Aren't you pleased?' he asked.

'Of course I'm pleased,' Lovell relented. 'But not why you think.'

Clarence frowned. 'Then why?'

Lovell stopped and pointed back at the great machine that lumbered behind them. 'Because,' he began with a conspiratorial smile, 'that bundle of nuts and bolts is the only one of us who knows where my gold is buried.'

OTHER GREAT TITLES
FROM ANDERSON ENTERTAINMENT

STINGRAY

Stingray: Operation Icecap

The Stingray crew discover an ancient diving bell that leads them on an expeditionary voyage through the freezing waters of Antarctica to the land of a lost civilisation. Close on the heels of Troy Tempest and the pride of the World Aquanaut Security Patrol is the evil undersea ruler Titan. Ahead of them are strange creatures who inhabit underground waterways and an otherworldly force with hidden powers strong enough to overwhelm even Stingray's defences.

Stingray: Monster from the Deep

Commander Shore's old enemy, Conrad Hagen, is out of prison and back on the loose with his beautiful but devious daughter, Helga. When they hijack a World Aquanaut Security Patrol vessel and kidnap Atlanta, it's up to Captain Troy Tempest and the crew of Stingray to save her. But first they will have to uncover the mystery of the treasure of Sanito Cathedral and escape the fury of the monster from the deep.

Thunderbirds: Operation Asteroids

What starts out as a simple rescue mission to save a trapped miner on the moon, soon turns out to be one of International Rescue's greatest catastrophes. After the Hood takes members of International Rescue hostage during the rescue, a chase across space and an altercation among the asteroids only worsens the situation. With the Hood hijacking Thunderbird Three along with Brains, Lady Penelope and Tin-Tin, it is up to the Tracy brothers to stage a daring rescue in the mountain tops of his hidden lair. But can they rescue Brains before his engineering genius is used for the destructive forces of evil?

Thunderbirds: Terror from the Stars

Thunderbird Five is attacked by an unknown enemy with uncanny powers. An unidentified object is tracked landing in the Gobi desert, but what's the connection? Scott Tracy races to the scene in the incredible Thunderbird One, but he cannot begin to imagine the terrible danger he is about to encounter. Alone in the barren wilderness, he is possessed by a malevolent intelligence and assigned a fiendish mission – one which, if successful, will have the most terrifying consequences for the entire world. International Rescue are about to face their most astounding adventure yet!

Thunderbirds: Peril in Peru

An early warning of disaster brings International Rescue to Peru to assist in relief efforts following a series of earth tremors – and sends the Thunderbirds in search of an ancient Inca treasure trove hidden beneath a long-lost temple deep in the South American jungle! When Lady Penelope is kidnapped by sinister treasure hunters, Scott Tracy and Parker are soon hot on their trail. Along the way they'll have to solve a centuries-old mystery, brave the inhospitable wilderness of the jungle and even tangle with a lost tribe – with the evil Hood close behind them all the way...

Intergalactic Rescue 4: Stellar Patrol

It is the 22nd century. The League of Planets has tasked Jason Stone, Anne Warran and their two robots, Alpha and Zeta to explore the galaxy, bringing hope to those in need of rescue. On board Intergalactic Rescue 4, they travel to ice moons and jungle planets in 10 exciting adventures that see them journey further across the stars than anyone before. But what are the secret transmissions that Anne discovers? And why do their rescues seem to be taking them on a predetermined course? Soon, Anne discovers that her co-pilot, Jason, might be on a quest of his own...

SPACE: 1999 Maybe There –
The Lost Stories from SPACE: 1999

Strap into your Moon Ship and prepare for a trip to an alternate universe!

Gathered here for the first time are the original stories written in the early days of production on the internationally acclaimed television series SPACE: 1999. Uncover the differences between Gerry and Sylvia Anderson's original story Zero G, George Bellak's first draft of The Void Ahead and Christopher Penfold's uncredited shooting script Turning Point. Each of these tales shows the evolution of the pilot episode with scenes and characters that never made it to the screen. Wonder at a tale that was NEVER filmed where the Alpha People, desperate to migrate to a new home, instigate a conflict between two alien races. Also included are Christopher Penfold's original storylines for Guardian of Piri and Dragon's Domain, an adaption of Keith Miles's early draft for All That Glisters and read how Art Wallace (Dark Shadows) originally envisioned the episode that became Matter of Life and Death.

Discover how SPACE: 1999 might have been had they gone 'Maybe There?'

available from
shop.gerryanderson.com

170